POINT OF KNIVES

"Scott returns to the intrigue-laden city of Astreiant in this novella, which bridges the gap between 1995's *Point of Hopes* and 2001's *Point of Dreams*.... Primarily an intriguing pseudo-police procedural, this fantasy also serves as a satisfying romantic story, with strong world building and great characterization that will leave readers wanting more."
—*Publishers Weekly*

"Blood, alchemy, sexual tension, murder, intrigue, and truly wonderful characters: Melissa Scott's *Point of Knives* delivers them all, in a world that seems so real, I'm surprised to look up and find I'm not living in it."
—Delia Sherman, author of *The Freedom Maze* and *The Porcelain Dove*

"Rathe and Eslingen are fascinating to follow as they navigate the deadly intrigues and dangerous magic of *Point of Knives*."
—Ginn Hale, author of *Wicked Gentlemen*

"The city of Astreiant with its complex loyalties and magics is one of the *realest* imaginary places I've had the privilege of visiting. An unlooked-for pleasure, then, to read a new adventure of pointsman Nicolas Rathe and out-of-work soldier Philip Eslingen. And what an adventure! Murdered pirates, royal and academic and metallurgical politics, wild guesses and careful detective work—and just the apt touch of romantic tension. *Point of Knives* is an engrossing addition to the small canon of fantastical mystery stories."
—Alex Jeffers, author of *You Will Meet a Stranger Far from Home*

"*Points of Knives* is gorgeous addition to the Astreiant series. Melissa Scott takes this fantasy, fills it with memorable characters, and gives the reader more by incorporating a fully developed romance and a police procedural with enough twists and turns to satisfy the most finicky of readers. Highly recommended."
—*Impressions of a Reader* blog

POINT OF KNIVES

※ A NOVELLA OF ASTREIANT ※

POINT OF KNIVES

MELISSA SCOTT

※ LETHE PRESS ※

Published in 2012 by Lethe Press, Inc.
118 Heritage Avenue ✦ Maple Shade, NJ 08052-3018
www.lethepressbooks.com ✦ lethepress@aol.com
ISBN: 1-59021-381-5
ISBN-13: 978-159021-381-0

This book is a work of fiction. Names, characters, places, and incidents
are products of the author's imaginations or are used fictitiously.

Set in Jenson and Ornatique.
Cover and interior design: Alex Jeffers.
Cover artwork: Ben Baldwin.

LIBRARY OF CONGRESS CATALOGING-IN-PUBLICATION DATA

Scott, Melissa.
  Point of knives : a novella of Astreiant / Melissa Scott.
    p. cm.
  ISBN 978-1-59021-381-0 (pbk. : alk. paper)
  1. Gay men--Fiction. 2. Murder--Investigation--Fiction. I. Title.
  PS3569.C672P67 2012
  813'.54--dc23
                        2012009418

FOR STEVE
Thanks for asking!

Chapter One
Bodies at Dawn

Nicolas Rathe dragged himself awake at the sound of fists on his door, groped for flint and steel and the candlestick beside the bed.

"Who's there?"

"Jiemen, Adjunct Point. You're wanted, sir."

Rathe suppressed a groan and got the candle lit, carried it to the table and went to open the door. The winter-sun was sinking, hidden behind the city's roofs, and the sky outside the open window was just beginning to show light in the east. "What time is it?"

"Half past five," Jiemen answered. She came into the narrow room, lantern in hand, set it on the table beside the candle, opening the slide to cast a better light. She'd been on the overnight shift, was dressed and ready, leather jerkin over a wool bodice and skirt, stout shoes showing at her hem. Truncheon and knife both hung ready at her belt.

Rathe reached for his breeches—there was no need to stand on ceremony with a fellow pointsman—and began to dress. The air from the window was chill, but it would warm up later on, two days past the Fall Balance, and he grabbed linen stockings instead of wool. "What's amiss?"

"It's Grandad Steen," Jiemen said, and Rathe's fingers stumbled on the buttons of his shirt.

"What?"

She nodded grimly. "Dame Lulli sent to us just past second sunset, said one of her boys had tripped over him in the yard. Murdered and robbed, she said."

"Damn." Rathe hastily wound his neckcloth to close his collar, and shrugged himself into his coat. Grandad Steen was one of the sights of Point of Hopes, claiming seventy-five years of age and a long career as a summer-sailor—a pirate—and if someone had killed him, it was probably because they'd been fool enough to believe his tales of lost treasure and distant islands where mermaids haunted the lagoons, kidnapping unwary sailors to father their finny children. Rathe'd asked once, when he was an apprentice, how they'd stolen the sailors without drowning them, and Grandad had spun him a story of eel-skin head-bags to hold the air, and houses half in, half out of the water, connected to the sea by underwater tunnels too long for any but a mermaid to swim…. Glorious nonsense, all of it, and a loss to the city, though he doubted he'd find too many others to agree. "Do we know when?"

Jiemen shrugged. "Not yet. Dame Lulli said she sent to us straightaway, and told off her knife to be sure things were left as they found them."

"Oh, she has a knife, does she?" Rathe found his tablets, slipped them into his pocket with his purse, and took his jerkin from its hook by the door.

"Not because she has a business to protect," Jiemen said, with vicious mimicry, "and certainly not because she's in the business of supplying certain ladies with suitable and fertile company—though that's in her mind practically a public service—because any such business would require her to be licensed and bonded, but only because she's giving him a job out of the kindness of her heart."

Rathe grinned in spite of himself. "I'm sure that will go over well in the courts. How many guests were there—poor ladies benighted whom the dame took in out of pure pity, I'm sure."

"I don't know." Jiemen saw that he was dressed, and picked up the lantern. "I sent Baiart on ahead."

"Good." Rathe hooked his truncheon onto his belt and blew out the candle. "Let's go."

The city of Astreiant was only just beginning to awaken, a few lamps showing in back kitchens and stableyards. They passed a pair of sleepy-looking live-out apprentices heading for the Hopes-Point bridge and their masters in Manufactory Point, and a few minutes later an empty cart overtook them, the driver sitting sideways on the tongue behind the plodding horse.

Jiemen looked sideways. "Oh, and I sent to the dead-house, too, Adjunct Point."

"Good."

Lulli's house was easy to pick out, the only one with all the doors open and lanterns and torches blazing in the yard. The neighbors were up, too, peeping out their windows, one or two substantial dames hovering in their doorways, but Rathe ignored them. Biatris Austor, the newest apprentice at Point of Hopes and so the one assigned to the overnight shift, was hovering at the alley gate, and swung it open at their approach.

"He's out back, ma'am and sir."

Rathe nodded, and looked at Jiemen. "Stay here and wait for the alchemists. And keep the neighbors away."

"Yes, Adjunct Point."

He didn't have to tell her to keep an eye out for anyone who was a little too interested in the business: they'd both been on the job long enough to know how often the murderer came back to check on her or his handiwork, and the more so when it was a killing as senseless as this one. He nodded again, and made his way down the narrow alley between the houses into Lulli's back garden.

She made good use of it, that much was clear. The fence was high and new, the privy recently whitewashed, posts ready to hang laundry and a thriving kitchen garden at the back step. Someone, Lulli or her cook, had set cloches over the more delicate herbs, trying to eke out a few more weeks' harvest before the frosts set in hard. Lulli herself was standing in the doorway, a scarlet wrapper thrown over her shift, blood-bright in the rising light. Her arms were folded across her chest, hugging herself hard even though the air was not so cold, and Rathe gentled his voice as he approached her. It seemed she had been fond of the old man, too.

"Dame Lulli."

She blinked at him from under her cap, and her frown eased a little. "It's Rathe, isn't it? The adjunct?"

"That's right." Rathe glanced over his shoulder, saw Baiart squatting by a shapeless lump that must be the body. He'd had the sense to fetch a blanket, covered it against the arrival of the alchemists from the deadhouse, and Rathe looked back at the woman. "Dame, I'll want to talk to you and to the household, but first I need to see the body. If you want to go in and make yourself a cup of tea—" Or something stronger, he added silently. "I won't need for you a little while yet."

"Thank you." From her voice she'd been weeping. "In a bit. Who'd do such a thing?"

"We'll find out," Rathe said, and turned to the body.

Baiart came to his feet at Rathe's approach, and shook his head. "A bad business, sir."

"Yeah." Rathe went to his knees, folded back the blanket. "You closed his eyes?"

"Yes, sir. I didn't touch anything else."

Rathe nodded. The old man lay all in a heap, legs bent one way, arms outflung, the front of his patched shirt drenched with blood. Stabbed and then searched, Rathe guessed: Grandad's coat was spread wide, the cuffs and hem slit, and the pockets of his breeches were pulled out. He looked up. "No purse?"

"No. They took his tobacco-pouch, too." Baiart lifted the lantern, trying to minimize the shadows, and Rathe gave a nod of thanks.

"And his hat, it looks like." Grandad usually wore a waterman's knit cap with a long tail, and sailors were known to keep a coin or two knotted in the fabric. "Do we know what he was doing up so early?"

"Dame Lulli says this was his usual time, more or less," Baiart answered. "He tends the stoves for the house."

Rathe nodded again, and eased the bloodied shirt open to get a look at the wound. A single stab wound, more or less to the heart—an up-and-under thrust, by the look of it, but not entirely expert. He lifted Grandad's right hand, cold and already stiffening, and wasn't surprised to see the knuckles bloodied. "No knife?"

"Not on him," Baiart said. "Seems to me he usually wore one, but I wouldn't swear to it. And at home—who knows?"

"He counted this as home?" Rathe rose to his feet again, scanning the beaten earth around the body.

"So Dame Lulli says."

There was a son, Rathe remembered, vaguely, and maybe a grandson, but he didn't know any more than that. He didn't know anything about the mother, but it wasn't that uncommon for a woman to leave an unintended son with his father rather than raising it herself. Had Grandad said something about that once, or was that just a part of one of his stories?

Another darker spot in the dirt beyond the body caught his eye, and he crouched to touch it warily. "Baiart?"

Baiart brought the lantern, and Rathe wiped his fingers on his handkerchief, unsurprised at the rusty stain. It could always be Grandad's, he thought, they wouldn't know for sure until the alchemists arrived, but he had a feeling....

"Give me the light," he said, and Baiart handed him the lantern. Rathe held it high, looking for more signs. Sure enough, there was a larger pool by the body, but the first spot he'd found was well separated, and there was a scuffed place in the dirt, not quite a footprint. And then he saw a second spot, and a third, leading toward the mews-gate, and he looked back at Baiart. "I've got a trail."

"I'll go with you," Baiart said.

Rathe shook his head. "Stay here, wait for whoever the deadhouse sends. I doubt it'll go far, but...." He squinted at the sky, lightening further as sunrise approached. "I want to get as far as I can before it's muddled. Tell Dame Lulli I'll be back to speak with her, though."

"Yes, sir," Baiart said.

Rathe let himself out into the narrow mews. It was a short lane, bounded on both sides by high fences, and the ground was soft, rutted from the night-soil carts and the the rag-and-bone women, but he could still pick out the blood trail. It led him out of the mews and and down the side street that ran parallel to Bridge Street, toward the maze of little shops and warehouses that lined the river's edge. That made it seem even more likely that it was someone who'd believed Grandad's tales of piracy, and Rathe hoped there would be a simple end to the case. Grandad deserved better than this.

The light was better in the street, a good thing, since the trail was fading. Rathe lifted his lantern again, found the next mark, and then a scuffed place beyond it, as though the person had stumbled. Rathe frowned at that. It looked as though the attacker was worse hurt than he'd thought, and he quickened his step.

A few yards further on, there was a larger spot of blood, and when he looked up, there was a bloody smear on the whitewashed corner of the next building. He swore under his breath and drew his truncheon. The last thing he needed was to trap an injured murderer. But there was no help for it, no time to send for help. He opened the lantern's slide all the way, and stepped briskly around the corner.

At the end of the little alley, a man knelt beside a heap of old clothes that quickly resolved itself into a body. His hat was tipped to hide his face, but it was obvious that he was about to go through the fallen man's pockets.

"Hold hard," Rathe said, but the next words died in his throat as the kneeling man turned. "Eslingen?"

"Oh. Hello, Nico." Philip Eslingen sounded more sheepish than anything as he pushed himself to his feet. "I might have known it would be you."

"What are you doing?" Rathe asked. He refused to be distracted by his liking for the man. They had worked well together over the summer, when they'd hunted down the city's stolen children, and slept together more than once in the heady aftermath of that success, but they served incompatible masters, and had, reluctantly, agreed to part. And that was where the matter had to rest, whether he liked it or not.

"I've found a dead man," Eslingen answered, his voice suddenly sober. "Old Steen's all the name I know."

"What?" Rathe checked, startled, then moved in so that the light fell squarely on the body. That was the last thing he'd expected, to come chasing Grandad's murderer, and find instead his dead son. But it was Old Steen all right, lean and wiry, cap missing and his lank brown hair trailing in the mud. He was a man well known to the points and even better to the pontoises who had jurisdiction over the river, but he'd never been on bad terms with his father, was said to bring him the occasional treat from the Silklands and the Further North.

"Shot with a bird-bolt," Eslingen said. "And either left to die, or got away."

"Got away, I think," Rathe said, the pieces slotting into place. If someone had been after Old Steen—that made more sense, even if it meant that Grandad's murder was an afterthought, someone covering her tracks. If Old Steen had been visiting his father when he was shot— He shook himself. "Philip, what are you doing here?"

"Caiazzo's business," Eslingen answered, and Rathe made a face. Of course it was, Hanselin Caiazzo being master of a lunar dozen businesses of just the sort of questionable legality that would lead to meetings in the dead of night, and it didn't make it any better that he, Rathe, had been the one to find Eslingen the position as Caiazzo's knife. It didn't matter that he'd needed Eslingen's help then—it had been at the height of the child-thefts, and he'd been desperate for any clue—or that he hadn't realized then quite how much he'd come to like the Leaguer. He'd made his bed, and would have to lie on it: a pointsman could not afford too close a friendship with Caiazzo's knife.

Eslingen took his silence for disapproval. "I can't tell you much, Nico, you know that. I was supposed to meet him at the Bay Tree, but he didn't show. I waited a bit, and then when it was getting on to sunrise, I came out to see what was what before I went back to Customs Point. And found him here."

Rathe nodded, unaccountably relieved. "They'll vouch for you at the Bay Tree, then?"

"They will." Eslingen didn't seem offended, thankfully, but then, being Caiazzo's man had left him inured to suspicion. Or maybe that was just being a soldier in a city notorious for its unmartial attitudes. "But why are you here, Nico? And before anyone's sent for you."

"I came from his father's body," Rathe said. "Someone stabbed Grandad Steen, and then presumably shot Old Steen—or maybe it was the other way around, but in any case, I followed a blood trail here." He sighed. "Grandad's hands were marked. He'd fought, and I hoped I was trailing his killer."

"The father dead, too?" Eslingen shook his head. "I didn't know he had one—living, that is, or anyway one he knew. You know what I mean."

"I do. There were three of them, Grandad and Old Steen, and his boy, Young Steen, all sailors—summer-sailors, according to rumor."

Eslingen tipped his head in question.

"That's pirates to you," Rathe said. "Or so the rumor went. Motherless men, all three of them, but no worse than many."

"I'm a motherless man myself," Eslingen said, a little too lightly.

Rathe winced, but it was too late to apologize. "Well," he said, and knelt beside the body. "Hold the lantern, will you?"

Eslingen did as he was told, opening the shutter and tilting the light so that it fell from the side, minimizing the shadows. The day-sun would be rising by now, but the alley was still deep in shadow. Rathe reached for the edge of Old Steen's coat—it was fancy, long-skirted, expensive braid still neatly stitched at hem and cuffs—and something growled at him. Beside him, Eslingen swore, and the skirts bunched and shifted, the growl increasing.

"Easy, now," Rathe said, and a head poked from beneath the cloth, fierce brown eyes above a pointed muzzle, teeth bared. "Easy."

"What in Seidos' name?" Eslingen began.

The dog wriggled free of the coat, backed itself between the body and the wall, hackles up and teeth still showing white in the lantern-light. It was tiny, not much bigger than a two-pound loaf of bread, with a shaggy black coat and pointed ears and no tail at all.

"It's a little-captain," Rathe said. He extended his hand cautiously, not so far that the dog could bite, but close enough that it could get the scent of him. "They're a river breed, meant to guard the barges."

"That's a guard dog?" Eslingen said, dubiously, and in spite of everything, Rathe grinned.

"Depends on where he latches on, doesn't it?"

Eslingen shifted, but to his credit didn't step back. "I'll assume you just mean ankles."

"You do that." Rathe kept his hand extended. "Hello, small dog, Steen's dog. No one's going to hurt you, pup."

The little-captain flung back his head and let out a piercing howl.

Eslingen winced. "I begin to see their uses."

"Yeah." Rathe stood, truncheon displayed now as a badge of office, as windows opened all along the alley. "Points business!" he called. "Who'll earn a demming carrying word to Point of Hopes?"

There was a scuffling from the head of the alley, and a girl appeared. "I'll go."

"Ask for Chief Point Monteia," Rathe said. "Tell her there's another body, and to send to the dead-house."

"Another body and send to the dead-house," the girl repeated. "Yes, sir."

She scampered off, and Rathe looked as Eslingen.

"I don't suppose your credit at the Bay Tree extends as far as a collar and leash?"

"I imagine they can provide," Eslingen answered. "But—favor for favor, Nico? I'd like to be there when you examine the body."

Rathe hesitated. It was far too easy to fall into old habits, the way they'd worked together over the summer, when they'd rescued the stolen children together—and after, when they'd fit all too well, in bed and out. But whatever was going on now, Caiazzo was up to his neck in it, and the Surintendant of Points had been wanting to call a solid point on him for more than a decade. "One thing first," he said. "Spread your arms."

Eslingen paused. "I'm no archer," he said, but lifted his arms from his side so that his coat fell open over his waistcoat and shirt. Rathe could see there was no standard crossbow concealed beneath the fine wool, but stepped closer anyway, ran his hands along the other man's ribs. Eslingen caught his breath.

"Now you're just being—difficult."

"Don't you want me to be able to swear you had nothing to do with this?" Rathe glanced quickly around but there was no place in the alley to hide even the smallest of crossbows.

"You can keep looking if you want," Eslingen offered. "Wouldn't want to miss anything."

"Later, maybe," Rathe said, with a certain amount of regret, and Eslingen shook himself.

"Right, sorry. Leash and a collar, you said?"

"A leash, anyway," Rathe answered. In the rising light, he could see that the little-captain had a collar already, well-worn studded leather. "Or a rope. Anything like that." He paused, sure he was going to regret this. "And then, yeah, you can come to the dead-house with me."

IN THE FOUR months he'd been in Astreiant, Eslingen had had no reason to visit the city's dead-house, and couldn't say even now that the idea particularly appealed to him. It was especially unappealing after an exceptionally early morning, trailing the alchemists' cart across the fog-wreathed Hopes-Point bridge and across the city to the border the University shared with the manufactory district. The river fog was burning off now that the sun was fully up, the cobbles damp and slick underfoot, and he stifled a yawn. Rathe, walking a little ahead of him so that he could talk quietly to one of the apprentices, looked as though he got up before sunrise every day. Which he easily could, Eslingen thought. It was more startling than he liked to realize how little he really knew about the man. Except that he was good with dogs: the little-captain was following quietly now at the end of his leash, not happy, but recognizing authority.

Eslingen shook his head. He refused to regret his choices—if, indeed, you could call them choices at all. Leaguers like himself had been the first people suspected when children started disappearing from the city's streets; Rathe had not only defended him, but found him a place when he'd lost his, and even if that had been as much to make Rathe's own job easier, Eslingen had been, and still was, grateful. Except that Caiazzo had two fingers in nearly every questionable business dealing in his home neighborhood of Customs Point, and had made it clear that Eslingen would have to choose between his position and his growing affair with Nicolas Rathe. Caiazzo's knife could not be in bed with the points, in any sense of the words. Probably he should have left Caiazzo's service, but that would have meant leaving Astreiant altogether, and that—well, it would have put paid to any chance of seeing Rathe again. Better to drift a little longer, and see what turned up, or so he'd kept telling himself. This dead man, however, wasn't quite what he'd had in mind.

The dead-house was a long low building with nothing to distinguish it from the other, similar buildings around it except the mage-lights in its windows and the air of quiet bustle already surrounding it. The apprentices brought the cart around toward a back door, but Rathe caught his sleeve when he would have followed.

"We can use the front door."

"Generous of them," Eslingen said, but followed obediently.

There was no smell at all, that was the thing he noticed most. The walls and floor were stone laid so tight Eslingen doubted you could slide a slip of paper into the gap, and everything was scoured spotless. A trio of apprentices were washing the far end of the hall, one sluicing the stones, the others driving the water ahead of them with heavy brooms, but all it did was make Eslingen think of the smells that weren't there. He'd seen dead men in plenty, having been a soldier since he was fourteen, had done his share of burial detail, and this cleanliness felt unnatural.

Rathe clearly knew his way around the place, as of course a pointsman would. He stooped to tuck the little-captain under his arm, then steered them down a series of halls, finally knocking on a heavy iron-bound door. It opened at once, and a plump homely woman peered out, wiping her hands on her apron.

"Hello, Nico," she said. "Are these yours?"

Rathe nodded. "Afraid so. And I'm going to need answers in a hurry. I have a feeling this one's going to be ugly."

"So I see," she answered. "I was born in Point of Knives, I knew Grandad and his stories."

"Thanks," Rathe said, with what sounded like relief. "Cas, this is Philip Eslingen. He's with me for now. Philip, this is Nianne Castera."

"Magist," Eslingen murmured, and she nodded briskly in answer.

"Who'd want to kill the old man?" Castera pulled the door open fully, beckoned them inside. Eslingen braced himself, and followed.

The bodies were already stripped, laid out on a pair of stone tables, and a curly-headed boy was just sorting their clothes into two neat piles. The air was more than naturally chill, and still utterly without scent. Eslingen took a step closer to the table that held Old Steen's belongings, and Rathe gave him a sharp look.

"Something particular you're looking for?"

Eslingen gave him his best smile. "Not really, no." From the lift of Rathe's eyebrow, he didn't believe that for an instant, and Eslingen couldn't really blame him. But in point of fact, the things he'd been expecting, the things he'd been sent to fetch, had clearly never been on the man. Caiazzo wouldn't be happy that his man was dead, but he'd be even less happy at the possibility that he was being cheated.

"There's not much," the boy said, misunderstanding, "Just the usual."

"Less than that, I'd say," Rathe said, frowning. He glanced at Eslingen. "We wouldn't be looking for letters or anything like that, would we?"

"Not on my account," Eslingen answered, with perfect truth. "Or not that I know of, anyway."

"Don't tell me Hanselin doesn't trust you," Rathe said.

"He feels my provenance to be doubtful," Eslingen said, and won a smile.

"I suppose he might, at that."

"Your recommendation is a double-edged sword, Adjunct Point," Eslingen said.

The little-captain chose that moment to give another mournful howl, and everyone jumped. "Sorry," Rathe said, and gentled it to silence. He looked back at Eslingen. "Grandad was searched pretty thoroughly. What about Old Steen?"

"I don't think so," Eslingen said. "He wasn't very cold when I found him, and I think I was first there."

"I'd agree," Castera said. "There's his purse still on him, and a knife, and quite a nice pipe. And his keys." She stood back, hands on hips, studying Old Steen's body. The boy was sponging it clean, but the birdbolt still jutted between the ribs, the flesh torn and purpled around it. "And he didn't die straightaway. The bolt took him turning, I'd say, and he ran—is that his dog? Maybe it distracted the killer. And then he kept moving, trying to escape, trying to get somewhere safe, until his heart gave out and he died."

Eslingen shivered at the images she conjured. Alchemists were masters of transformation, they could read the changes in an object and track them to their source, that was why they were guardians of the dead. But it wasn't a comfortable talent. He glanced at the other body, the old man—another Steen, Rathe had said, Old Steen's father. The boy had done his best to make him presentable, but the stab wound below the breast was still ugly. And not, Eslingen thought, with sharpening attention, what he would have expected. Oh, it was effective enough, but it wasn't expert, and most of the knives and bravos who meddled in Caiazzo's business were nothing but expert.

"You noticed that," Rathe said in his ear, and Eslingen lifted an eyebrow.

"Noticed what?"

"Whoever stabbed him was no professional," Rathe said. "Just like whoever shot Old Steen didn't make it count. Does that mean anything to you?"

"There's only so much I can tell you, Nico," Eslingen said. He chose his words with care. "Caiazzo sent me to meet Old Steen, by way of business, and that's all I can say about that. But he wasn't expecting trouble, nor was I, and if there were going to be trouble in this business, I wouldn't expect to find the bodies at all."

Rathe made a face, but nodded, the little-captain squirming again under his arm. "What about Grandad?" he asked, and Castera looked up from contemplating the body.

"He fought, though I'm sure you saw that yourself. I'd say he had a knife of his own, from the marks on his hands, but he was an old man, for all his talk. It wouldn't take too much strength to beat past his guard." Her mouth tightened for a moment. "He died about the same time his son was shot, and, being that they're father and son and the bodies found not too far apart, I'd be inclined to say they were attacked in the same place."

"But there's nothing alchemical to say that," Rathe said, and Castera shook her head.

"Sadly, no. Two different weapons, otherwise I could say yea or nay. And different enough that I can't even say if it's a similar hand. At least not by alchemy."

Rathe nodded. "Hold them for me, will you? And do a full autopsy?"

"Rathe, the cause of death is entirely clear," Castera said.

"Humor me?" he asked, and after a moment she shrugged and nodded. "All right. But I doubt I'll find more than I've already told you."

"There's something not right here," Rathe answered. "With your permission, Cas, I'll take their belongings back to Point of Hopes, and put out a cry for the next-of-kin."

"D'you have the list?" she said, to the boy, and he nodded. "Right, then. Sign for them, Rathe, and they're all yours. And—good luck. Grandad was a worthless old sot, but he didn't deserve this."

Rathe checked the list, and scribbled his name and title at the bottom, then tucked the bundle into the pocket opposite the little-captain. The dog struggled as they left, yelping and whining, but once they were out in the street, it settled to a morose silence. Eslingen adjusted his hat, shading his eyes from the rising sun.

"I'm for Customs Point," he said, and Rathe shook his head.

"Sorry, Philip. You'll need to give us your story."

"I've given it to you," Eslingen protested. "Have a heart, Nico, I've been up most of the night."

"I'm sure you'll manage," Rathe answered, and Eslingen followed.

THE SUN WAS fully up by the time they reached the station square at Point of Hopes, the streets waking to the routines of the day. A flock of gargoyles scolded from the midden beside a bakery, and a sleepy-looking apprentice was washing the steps of the inn at the corner. There was a a bustle of activity in the station's main room, the night-watch handing over to the day, and Eslingen checked just inside the doorway, not wanting to be in the way. Rathe ignored it, and hung cap and jerkin on the waiting hooks. The little-captain hovered at his ankles, wary but not yet growling.

"Is the chief in yet?" he asked, to no one in particular, and a blonde woman straightened from the duty point's table, where she'd been studying a ledger.

"Not yet, Adjunct Point. She's on her way."

"Good." Rathe worked his shoulders, then picked up the dog, settling it into the crook of his arm. "There's been two murders on the edge of Point of Knives, probably related—it's Grandad Steen and his son."

The blonde frowned. "Why would anyone kill Grandad, for Sophia's sake?"

Rathe looked at Eslingen. "I intend to find out. And have one of the runners make us some tea."

"Right, Adjunct Point." The blonde reached for a pen and a scrap of paper, began scribbling.

Breakfast would be nice, too, Eslingen thought, but he wasn't sure enough of Rathe's mood to say it aloud.

The blonde finished her note, handed it to one of the waiting runners, and sent another one to the station's well to fill Rathe's kettle. "I heard that Young Steen's ship came in yesterday," she said. "Should we send for him, too?"

"Now, that's interesting," Rathe said. "Yeah, let him know. I imagine he's the one to claim the bodies, but if not, he'll know who is." He looked over his shoulder. "In the meantime, Eslingen—you and I need to have a talk."

"I'm at your disposal, Adjunct Point," Eslingen murmured, and followed him up the stairs.

He still hadn't figured out exactly what he was going to tell Rathe, and Rathe didn't give him any time to consider, either, just pointed to the spare chair and settled himself behind his table. He set the little-captain on the table-top, and it padded back and forth across the scattered papers before settling itself with an almost human sigh.

"Right," Rathe said. "What exactly were you doing at the Bay Tree, Philip?"

"A job for Caiazzo," Eslingen answered.

"I'd got that far," Rathe said, with a crooked grin. "Could you be a bit more specific?"

"Old Steen was supposed to have a packet for Caiazzo," Eslingen said. "I was supposed to collect it, the thought being that sending me was more discreet than having Old Steen come to the house, or for Caiazzo to go to him. Only he didn't arrive as arranged, and when I finally gave up waiting, I practically tripped over his body."

"Not at the end of a blind alley, you didn't," Rathe said.

"Metaphorically," Eslingen said. "I told you, I looked around a bit to see if I could find out what had gone wrong." He shook his head as a runner appeared with the pot of tea. "I really didn't expect to find him dead. It wasn't that sort of job at all."

"What sort of job was it?" Rather asked, and jammed a hand into his hair. "No, wait, don't answer that! Unless—is it something I need to know?"

"Not in the least," Eslingen answered promptly, and Rathe grinned.

"I'll let that pass for now. Pour us some tea, will you?"

Eslingen found the woven-wicker strainer and obliged, filling a pair of cheap pottery cups. He handed one to Rathe and took the other for himself, wrapping his fingers around the heating surface. "Seriously, Nico, I wasn't expecting any trouble. Caiazzo wasn't expecting trouble. I'd have come better armed if he had been."

"So why, then?" Rathe sipped cautiously at his tea. "Why kill not only your man but his aged father?"

"Damned if I know," Eslingen said. "Something personal, maybe?"

Rathe smiled. "That's always possible. But you'll forgive me if having Hanse involved makes me just a bit—wary."

"Caiazzo wouldn't kill him," Eslingen said. "He was buying—goods, shall we say? A straightforward piece of business."

"If outside the law," Rathe said, and Eslingen gave him a limpid stare.

"You know I can't answer that, Adjunct Point."

"Not that you need to," Rathe said.

Eslingen laughed. "Touché."

Rathe shook himself. "All right, I'll buy that. But if it's not because of Caiazzo's business—what, then?"

Eslingen rubbed his neck, the ache of a sleepless night settling into his bones. "It might—and I stress the word *might*, as in only possibly and remotely—have something to do with the business. Someone wanting to muscle in. But it wasn't expected, and Caiazzo didn't kill him."

Rathe shook his head, but he was smiling again. "Right. I'll bear that in mind, too: a mysterious something that might possibly have provoked someone to try to muscle in? That's very helpful, Philip."

"I try," Eslingen said, with exaggerated modesty, but sobered quickly. "I'll ask around, if you'd like. Caiazzo will want this person caught, if only as a lesson, so he might be willing to help."

"I'd appreciate it," Rathe said, and looked up as the door opened. The little-captain sat up just as sharply, brown eyes alert. "What is it, Lennar?"

"Excuse me, Adjunct Point, but Young Steen's here. About his father's body."

"Show him up," Rathe said. Eslingen started to rise, but Rathe waved for him to sit. "Stay," he said. "You can speak for Caiazzo if need be."

That was a double-edged sword, too, Eslingen thought, and sank back into his chair.

The man who appeared in the doorway was tall and sun-browned, his long hair bleached to the color of straw. He was younger than he looked at first sight—the lines around his eyes were carved by weather, not age— and he wore a decent coat over sailor's wide breeches, with a kerchief of bright Silklands printing to close the neck of his shirt. The little-captain scrambled to its feet at the sight of him, and launched itself into his arms. The sailor caught him with a fond curse, submitted to being licked on chin and nose before tucking the dog firmly into the crook of his arm.

"There's one question I don't have to ask," Rathe said, with a wry smile. "You'd be Old Steen's son."

The sailor nodded. "They call me Young Steen. I'm master of the *Soeuraine of Bedarres*." He glanced at the dog, still trying frantically to lick his face. "They tell me Dad's dead?"

"I'm sorry," Rathe said. "Yes."

"What happened?"

"He was shot with a birdbolt," Rathe said. "And—your grandfather was knifed as well."

"Dead?"

"I'm sorry," Rathe said again.

"Damn it to hell." Young Steen lifted the dog, buried his face in its fur. "Who—and why?"

"We don't know yet," Rathe said. "But we'll find out."

"Whatever fee—" Steen began, then shook his head. "No, I know you now. You're the one who doesn't take fees."

"I don't," Rathe said. From his tone, it was still a sensitive point—but then, Eslingen thought, most of Astreiant's pointsmen were happy to take an extra seiling or five to ensure a job well done. "What you can do is answer some questions."

"Yeah," Steen said. "Yes, of course." He glanced at Eslingen then, as though his presence had only just registered. "Who's this?"

"Philip Eslingen," Rathe answered. "He found your father's body."

"Oh, yes?" There was a definite note of suspicion in Young Steen's voice, and Eslingen straightened slightly.

"I was supposed to meet him, on my employer's behalf—Hanselin Caiazzo."

Steen nodded, not entirely appeased, looked back at Rathe. "You're sure of him?"

"I am," Rathe said, and Eslingen felt an unexpected warmth steal through him.

"Right." Steen took a deep breath, resettled the dog against his elbow. "What can I tell you?"

"Whatever you can," Rathe said. "Anything of his business, enemies, anyone you can think of who might have done this—or who might have it in for Grandad, for that matter. I've been assuming your father was the primary target, but I've no real proof of it."

Steen hissed softly through his teeth. "His business I don't know much of, or Grandad's. I've been at sea the last six months."

"But you knew he had dealings with Caiazzo," Rathe said.

"He'd done in the past," Steen answered. "It's no surprise to hear. Grandad, though, he's retired, he's got no business, except what he does for Dame Lulli, and that's his choice, Dad and me, we'd have taken care of him—" He broke off, shaking his head.

"Grandad's body was searched," Rathe said. "Any idea what someone might have been looking for?"

Steen shook his head again. "Grandad banked his money—Orlandi's, in Point of Sighs. Unless someone believed his stories? Tyrseis, that would be cruel."

"Stories?" Eslingen asked.

Steen looked at him. "Grandad liked to hang about the taverns and tell tales for drinks, about his life as a pirate and the like. There was always a lost treasure or three, and a mysterious island, and monsters." He broke off, blinking hard.

"Mermaids," Rathe said, and Steen looked blankly at him. "A story he told me once, and I've never forgotten. He'll be missed." He shook himself. "But I don't think that's why he was killed. Old Steen had business with Caiazzo, we know that much, and that's more likely to bring death in its wake."

Steen nodded slowly, his eyes on Eslingen. "And this business would be—?"

"Caiazzo's," Eslingen answered, carefully, and after a moment, Steen nodded again.

"I'll have a word with him, then, soldier."

"He'd welcome it, I think," Eslingen answered. Out of the corner of his eye, he saw Rathe grimace.

"And if it ends up having a bearing on these murders, I'd appreciate hearing it," he said. "Or I'll have to have a word with Hanse myself."

"And I'm sure that will please him, too," Eslingen murmured.

Rathe ignored him. "What about enemies? Anyone you can think of who'd want to kill your father?"

"Not so many ashore," Steen answered. "And not in Astreiant. He's only been home a week or two ahead of me—we both sail under charter from Bastian Souers, to the Silklands and the southern isles."

"So your guess would be that it was business?" Rathe asked, and Steen nodded.

"My first guess, anyway, Adjunct Point. But I don't know what he was up to since he was home."

"We'll be asking about that," Rathe said.

"Yeah." Steen squared his shoulder, the little-captain snuggling against him. "The—bodies. They'll be at the dead-house, then? How do I go about claiming them?"

"You'll need to prove you're the next-of kin," Rathe answered, "which shouldn't be a problem—"

He broke off at the knock at his door, tipped his head to one side. "I'm sorry, Adjunct Point," the runner Lennar said, "but Old Steen's wife is here to claim the body."

His eyes were wide at the very idea, and Eslingen blinked. Not many people of Old Steen's status ever married; they might run a shop or some other business with the woman whose bed they shared, whose children they fathered, or perhaps make some more tenuous contract, some promise of maintenance in exchange for the children and the company, but they did not marry. Not chartered captains who gave half their take to the women who funded the venture, and paid their crew out of their own share.

"My father's not married," Young Steen said.

"She has his marriage lines, the chief says," Lennar answered. "If you please, Adjunct Point?"

"Let's see what she has to say," Rathe said, forestalling Young Steen's indignant answer, and pointed him toward the door. He glanced back at Eslingen. "Come on, Philip, you don't want to miss the show."

"Indeed not," Eslingen answered, and trailed behind them down the stairs to the station's main room.

Chapter Two
The Summer-Sailor's Wife

RATHE LED THE way down the stairs, glad that Eslingen closed up at his shoulder, blocking Young Steen from any precipitate action. Monteia and Jiemen were standing beneath the station's case-clock, Jiemen looking harried, Monteia with her pipe in her mouth and her hands on her hips, staring at the third woman. She wasn't young herself, looked to be about the same age as Monteia, and as soberly dressed, bottle-green skirt and split-sleeved bodice that showed a glimpse of ivory linen. The neck was square but modest, made so by a fichu of inexpensive lace: not quite what he'd been expecting, and Rathe glanced over his shoulder at Young Steen.

"Do you know her?"

"I've never seen her before in my life."

Eslingen's eyebrows winged up at that, but he swallowed what was probably an inappropriate retort. Rathe gave him a look that he hoped conveyed the desire that Eslingen continue to behave decorously, and nodded to Monteia. "Chief?"

Monteia removed her pipe from her mouth, pointed with it to the stranger. "This is Costanze van Duiren, wife to Old Steen."

"No, she's not," Young Steen blurted.

"He never approved of the marriage," van Duiren said. Her voice was sharply southriver, less cultured than her clothes. "Him being motherless and all."

"There never was any marriage," Young Steen said. "In fact, I'd lay good money my father never even bedded you."

19

"Enough," Monteia said. "Captain, Dame van Duiren has your father's marriage lines."

"Forged, I don't know," Young Steen said. The little-captain, catching his mood, growled from the shelter of his arms.

"Unusual for the wife to have her husband's lines," Rathe observed. "Usually it's the man who wants the proof."

"He was at sea seven months out of twelve," van Duiren answered. "I kept many of his papers for him."

Out of the corner of his eye, Rathe saw Eslingen's head lift slightly. Whatever Caiazzo was after, then, there were papers involved. He put that thought aside for later. "I'd like to have a look at them, Chief?"

Monteia gestured with her pipe again, and van Duiren pulled the folded sheet from the purse at her waist, handing it over with a quiet flourish. Rathe took it, his gaze flicking over the printed form, the names and dates written in the familiar clerical hand, recording the marriage of Costanze van Duiren and Steen Stinson. There was a second document as well, a contract of maintenance, van Duiren's promise to support the potential father of her children should she conceive by him, with bonuses for a daughter, and the usual provisions for miscarriage and stillbirth. The ink had flowed smoothly, none of the faint shifts in color and thickness you saw on even competent forgeries, and all the stamps and seals looked genuine. He nodded and handed it back, and she folded it carefully away.

"The original of the contract is on file at the Temple, of course," she said. "I'll have that sworn to if necessary."

"We'll see," Monteia said.

"In any case," van Duiren said, "there can't be any serious argument that I'm not his next of kin. I am his wife, by all legal reckoning."

"You're not his wife," Young Steen said. "This is madness!"

"What proof do you have that there wasn't a marriage?" Monteia asked.

"My father wouldn't— I've never seen this woman before, never heard her name mentioned. Would my father marry and never tell his own son?"

"That's hardly proof," van Duiren said. "Even if it were true."

Young Steen took a step forward, and Eslingen blocked him without seeming to have moved at all.

"Dame van Duiren has a point," Monteia said.

"Ask his crew—ask his landlady," Young Steen began, and stopped, shaking his head. "Ask anyone who knew him."

"You can call your witnesses," Monteia said, and Young Steen shook his head again.

"I don't know who's in town, I don't even know where to start."

Rathe said, "What does the dog say?"

Monteia cocked her head at him, and Rathe held out his hand for the little-captain. Steen gave him up warily, and Rathe gentled it into the corner of his arm. "The dog should know her, right, if she's his wife."

"The dog didn't," van Duiren began, and stopped herself.

"Didn't what?" Monteia asked.

"Didn't like me," van Duiren said, with dignity. That wasn't what she'd intended to say, Rathe knew, but she'd saved herself from an outright lie.

"Let's see," he said, and set the little-captain on the polished stone. The dog turned in a rapid circle, then ran from shoe to shoe, looking up as if hoping one of them would be Old Steen. It treated Monteia no differently from van Duiren, though it barked once at Eslingen, then retreated to the shelter of Young Steen's ankles. The captain picked it up, glaring at Monteia.

"What more do you need? He doesn't know her. I doubt she even knows his name."

"Steen," van Duiren said, and the little-captain cocked his head, ears swiveling.

"Really?" Eslingen said, under his breath, and Rathe stepped back none too gently on his toe.

"It's an easy guess," Young Steen said.

Monteia shook her head. "Captain, if you can bring witnesses that your father was unmarried, I'd advise you to do so, and to pursue the matter in the courts. I don't see that I have any choice but to turn Old Steen's body over to Dame van Duiren. Subject, of course, to her paying the associated costs, as set out by the Chief Alchemist."

"But not Grandad," Young Steen said, and Monteia shook her head again.

"The claim passes from father to son, so there's no question you're his next-kinsman."

Rathe glanced quickly at van Duiren, but saw no change in her expression. Her business was entirely with Old Steen, then, which raised the odds that Grandad's death was unintentional.

"I'll take that charge gladly," Young Steen said. "And if she in any way defaults—I'll stand the charges, Chief Point."

"Duly noted," Monteia said. "Do I take it you mean to contest the marriage?"

Young Steen nodded. "I do."

"Then it's very likely the alchemists will hold his belongings until there's an order from the court," Monteia said.

"You're simply trying to drive up your fees," van Duiren said. "No judge would place the claim of a motherless man above a lawful wife."

"Lawful?" Young Steen's voice rose, and out of the corner of his eye, Rathe saw Eslingen pluck at his sleeve. The captain subsided slightly, the dog growling for him, a rising rumble of sound.

"That's for the court to decide," Monteia repeated. "Dame, I'll need one of the points to copy down the details of your papers."

And that, Rathe knew, was his cue to get Young Steen out of the station so there wouldn't be any more bloodshed in the streets. He turned toward him, but Eslingen already had a hand on Young Steen's elbow, and was steering him toward the door. Eslingen looked over his shoulder as though Rathe had called him, and winked. *Trust me*, he mouthed, and then they were gone. Rathe stood for a moment staring after them. He did trust Eslingen, that was the problem, even though he knew it probably wasn't safe. If only he hadn't found Eslingen the place in Caiazzo's household—but Eslingen had lost his previous post partly because of Rathe, and it had all seemed like a good idea at the time. And Eslingen had been a good companion during the hunt for the stolen children, always ready with a clever answer or an equally canny blow. And after— after it had been all too easy to fall into bed with him, and into a deepening friendship.

And this was definitely not the moment to be thinking about that. Old Steen's belongings were still in a bundle in his workroom: better to see what was there, and copy what he could, before van Duiren pressed her claim.

RATHE POURED HIMSELF another cup of the cooling tea, the early morning already beginning to wear on him, and closed the workroom door before he turned to the packet he'd been given at the dead-house. As Castera had said, it was clear that Old Steen hadn't been robbed: the untied bundle held the dead man's purse, still plump and clinking with coin, and his keys. Rathe set them aside for the moment, sorted quickly through the rest of the objects. It was the usual detritus of a working man's pockets, tinder-box, tobacco pouch and pipe—a nice one, polished briar inlaid with silver—a set of lead dice, a gnawed-on stylus, a quarter of a broadsheet prophecy and a few more scraps of paper twisted into spills, a silver storm-horse charm and a couple of thick hard-baked biscuits stamped with a running dog. Treats for the little-captain, Rathe knew, and set them aside. He tipped his head to one side, considering what was left. It was all very ordinary, though he wondered if the stylus meant that Old Steen was in the habit of carrying a set of wax tablets. There were none among the effects. He made a note to ask, and picked up the tobacco pouch. There was something hard in it, only partly masked by the loose herb, and he undid the strings, opening the pouch to its widest extent. Nestled among the shreds of tobacco was a single iron key the size of his thumb.

Rathe lifted his eyebrows—not the usual place to keep a key, certainly—and gently shook off the last of the oily strands. It looked ordinary enough, browned iron with plain-cut wards—castle-cut, he amended, looking at it more closely, and that meant a better lock than average. He would bet this was part of what Old Steen had been killed for.

He reached into the pocket of his own coat, brought out the wax tablets he always carried. They were empty, the wax planed smooth for the day, and he pressed the key carefully into the left-hand side, taking an impression of each face. In the back of his mind, he could hear Eslingen's voice, coolly amused—*you have unsuspected talents, Adjunct Point*—but put the thought aside. It was just as well to be able to make a copy of the keys, in case someone made Monteia give them up.

There was a knock at the door then, and he knotted the tobacco pouch closed, flipping the wrapping hastily over the various objects. "Yeah?"

Monteia pushed the door open, and Rathe relaxed slightly. "Hello, Chief."

"I thought you might have the effects," she said, and seated herself on the visitor's stool. "Van Duiren's gone to the dead-house, she'll be back here inside the hour, wanting them."

"Yeah," Rathe said again, and met her eyes without apology. "I needed time to look things over." He paused. "I thought you said the alchemists would keep them."

"The marriage lines look valid, and Young Steen hasn't yet filed a claim," Monteia said. "I doubt they'll argue." She paused. "What have you got?"

"Not much," Rathe answered. He spilled out the purse as he spoke, a handful of coins, mostly cooper demmings with a few rounds of silver among them, began counting as he spoke. "Pipe fittings, dice, dog-biscuit, his money and his keys."

"Definitely not robbed," Monteia said. "You said Grandad was searched?"

Rathe nodded. "There was nothing in his pockets, and purse and cap were missing. Maybe the killer thought Old Steen had given whatever it was she's looking for to Grandad? I don't know." He looked down at the note from the dead-house. "All told, he had two demmings less a pillar here, so, yeah, we can say he wasn't searched. That's too much money to leave behind. Though he's got a stylus here and no tablets, so I'll need to ask around about that."

"Common enough to have a stylus in the kit," Monteia said. "I use mine to clean my pipe." She reached across the desk, picked up the battered slip of bone to display the darkened tip. "Looks like Old Steen did the same."

Rathe nodded. "That makes sense. Thanks, Chief."

"Almost a pillar," Monteia said. "Two weeks keeping, that is, for most of us. Do we know where he lodged?"

"Not yet."

"I'd like to know," she said. "And before van Duiren has a chance to muddy the waters."

"You don't seriously think she married him, do you?" Rathe asked.

Monteia shook her head. "If she did, then I'm a Regent. And you don't see me sitting in All-Guilds, do you?"

"Then you wouldn't have any objection if I took an impression of his keys?" Rathe asked.

Monteia hesitated. "We've no right," she said at last. "And she's the sort to claim the letter of the law."

"It's murder," Rathe said, without much hope, and Monteia shook her head.

"I can't say yes to it. I'm sorry, Nico."

But she wasn't saying no, either. Rathe nodded in perfect understanding, and Monteia pushed herself to her feet.

"When you're done, I'll put these in the station strongbox. And one thing more."

Rathe gave her a wary look.

"I know you're fond of Eslingen, but he's Caiazzo's man. You can't trust him in this business."

"He did us—the points and the city—good service this summer," Rathe said.

"That was to save his own skin and Caiazzo's," Monteia said.

"I put him into Caiazzo's service, remember," Rathe said.

"So you did. And you'd better learn to live with it." She paused. "Don't force me to make it an order, Nico."

"I'll do my best, Chief," Rathe said, and the door closed behind her.

He kept a block of beeswax in his cabinet for just this purpose, and set it to warm in the sun while he looked over the ring of keys. Monteia was wrong about Eslingen, he was sure of that, though he couldn't have said precisely why. Or, rather, he could say it, could quote all the times during the search for the children that Eslingen had chosen their interests over Caiazzo's, the way he'd risked arrest and injury and finally his life, but he knew that he would only sound besotted. And I'm not, he thought. Not besotted. Fond of him, friendly with him—gods, it was easy to slip into the habit of the summer, too easy to treat him as comrade and friend—and if he was honest with himself, yes, he could become besotted. Could even— He refused to utter the betraying verb, even in his own mind. Wanted him still, yes, he'd admit that much because half the station felt the same way: Eslingen was an extraordinarily handsome man, with his pale skin and black hair and his vivid blue eyes. Liked him, too, and that was the heart of the trouble. No matter how much he liked and trusted Eslingen, he couldn't afford to give Caiazzo that much of an advantage. Monteia was right, he'd have to learn to live with it.

THEY WERE IN the station courtyard before Young Steen jerked his arm free of Eslingen's hand, and rounded on him with a glare.

"Not here," Eslingen said, and the logic of that was enough to carry them through the station's gate and out into the street.

"And who are you—"

"And not here, either," Eslingen said, "not unless you want everyone in Point of Hopes to know your affairs."

Steen scowled, but the point was unarguable. "Where, then? Because you and I have things to talk about, soldier."

"Lieutenant," Eslingen said, with a smile he didn't feel. He didn't really feel like claiming rank, either, but he suspected it was the best way to get Young Steen to follow quietly. "The Hare and Hawker?"

It was a tavern not far away, one that catered to travelers and therefore asked no questions. "I don't have time for this," Steen muttered, but nodded.

Eslingen steered them to a table in the corner, ordered tea and a cheese tart. Steen started to wave the potboy away, then visibly thought better of it and called for sausage and small beer.

"And an explanation," he added, looking at Eslingen. "What exactly was your business with Dad, Lieutenant?"

"I'm Caiazzo's knife," Eslingen said. It was the catchall Astreianter term for bodyguard, hired thug, or blade for hire. "He had business with your father, and sent me to handle it."

"What kind of business?" Steen's glare sharpened again.

"Not what you're thinking," Eslingen answered. "Old Steen had a cargo he wanted to dispose of discreetly—my impression was it hadn't paid the Queen's taxes, though it wasn't my place to know any details—and Caiazzo wanted to buy. I was to fetch a sample of the goods in exchange for a crown in silver."

Young Steen swore under his breath. "So that's—did Caiazzo tell you what the cargo was, Lieutenant?"

Eslingen shook his head. "He said I didn't need to know."

"He would." Young Steen showed teeth in a distinctly feral smile. "Dad wasn't here this summer, he was all the way south past the Outer Isles. He went to fetch his takings from three years past—gold, Lieutenant, coin of three realms, taken off the—wreck—of a Silklands hoy. A sea-chest full of gold, and none to claim it."

And doubtless Old Steen had been responsible for that wreck, Eslingen thought. He said, "The Queen takes her tithe of all gold, coin, nugget, ingot, or flakes and dust. It's the royal metal, there's a magistical link to her rule that has to be propitiated. Not to mention she's sensitive about it after this past summer." A crazed magist had stolen the city's children to mine aurichalcum, queen's-gold, that he intended to use to influence the succession and become the power behind Astreiant's throne: the queen and her agents were still keeping a very close eye on the banks and traders.

"Yeah. But Dad didn't know," Steen said. "If he had, he'd have left it another season."

And Caiazzo still needed gold, Eslingen thought, the pieces slotting into place at last. He'd lost his ready coin in the summer chaos, still had caravans to fund and less-legal businesses to support, and the last, in particular, dealt in cash, not letters of credit. Of course Caiazzo had jumped at the chance to change silver for gold, and of course Old Steen had been glad to take legal coin for untaxed, unworkable gold that he couldn't easily explain....

"And now that miserable bitch is going to claim Dad's goods," Young Steen said. "The gold along with it."

"Rathe doesn't believe her," Eslingen said. "He'll delay as long as possible. Which means you should call up those witnesses you spoke of—his crew, his friends, anyone who can speak to the matter—and haul them down to the station or get a sworn statement or both. That'll slow things down, at the very least."

"Why should the pointsman care?" Steen tossed down the last of his beer.

"Because it's justice," Eslingen said, and shrugged. "His stars run that way, I suppose, but—that's how he is. He's the man who saved the children, and he did it because someone had to."

"And I know you, now, too," Young Steen said, slowly. "You worked with him—you're the other half of that, Lieutenant."

"I helped," Eslingen said. "But it was Nico—Rathe—who did most of it."

"I'll call up my witnesses," Young Steen said. "And would you take a word to Caiazzo?"

"Of course."

"Tell him that if I can claim my father's goods, I'd be happy to make the same bargain with him that Dad did." Young Steen pushed himself to his feet, and Eslingen copied him, tossing a handful of demmings on the tabletop to cover the cost of the meal. Of course Young Steen would say that; it was the best way to get Caiazzo to back his claim. But it was also obvious that van Duiren was a liar—and probably after the gold herself, Eslingen thought.

"I'll tell him that," he said, and made his way through the tables to the door.

He caught a low-flyer back to Customs Point, paid it off at the bottom of the street where Caiazzo had his house, and went in by the side door, hoping to steal a moment to pull his thoughts together before he had to take his news to Caiazzo. Unfortunately, his wish was not granted. Aicelin Denizard, Caiazzo's magist and left hand, was crossing the hall as the door opened, and stopped in her tracks.

"Eslingen! You were looked for hours ago."

"I know," Eslingen answered. "Is himself about?"

"Above in his workroom, and contemplating sending runners to find you," Denizard answered. "I'll send him word you're here."

"Come up with me," Eslingen said. "You'll want to hear as well."

She lifted an eyebrow at that, but turned, the heavy grey silk of her magist's robe rustling against her fashionable ox-blood gown, and led the way up the central stairs.

Caiazzo's workroom was at the end of the gallery, with long windows like the stern of a ship overlooking the garden behind the house. His counter ran along the wall beneath it, piled with papers and ledgers and an abacus, and Caiazzo himself sat on a high stool near its center, while his clerk sat at a low table, diligently making notes. He broke off as the door opened, and the clerk looked up, pen poised.

"All right, Biblis, that'll be all for now," Caiazzo said. "Philip, I hope you have a good explanation for where you've been."

The clerk stoppered her inkwell and hurried out, Denizard closing the door firmly behind her. Eslingen took a breath. "I have an explanation," he said, "but I wouldn't call it good."

"Go on."

"Old Steen's dead," Eslingen said bluntly. "And his aged father murdered, too." He ran through the events of the previous night and their aftermath, finishing with Young Steen's offer. Caiazzo stared at him for a long moment, and Eslingen fought back the temptation to elaborate. That was one of Caiazzo's favorite tricks, luring you into saying more than you'd meant, and he refused to fall victim.

"So you've been at Point of Hopes all this time," Caiazzo said at last.

"Yes."

"What does Rathe say about the woman?"

"He doesn't believe she's his wife," Eslingen answered. "I don't think the Chief Point does, either, but the marriage lines look good."

"Oh, Bonfortune." Caiazzo slanted a reproachful glance at the altar hanging on the side wall, where a bright bundle of autumn flowers lay beneath the feet of the merchant-venturers' god, then slid from his stool. Standing, he was smaller than one might expect, a neat dark man, unobtrusively well dressed, with eyes that looked almost black in the morning light. Only the small scar at the corner of his mouth betrayed that he was more dangerous than he seemed. "Aice, I'll want my advocates on this straightaway. Have Lunele place a claim against the estate, that should tie things up for a bit."

Denizard nodded. "Do we have a claim?"

"Does it matter? She can find one, I'm sure." Caiazzo didn't wait for her answer, but reached for a pen and a clean sheet of paper. "As for you, Philip.... This is a note for the chief at Point of Hopes, what's her name—"

"Monteia," Eslingen said.

"Right, Monteia, stating that I'm making a claim, and that she'll be in receipt of a proper writ within the day." Caiazzo wrote busily for a few moments, the pen loud in the silence, then dusted the sheet with sand to dry the ink. "But your main business—I know you're still friends with Nicolas Rathe, and I'm pleased that you've not made it an issue for me.

And now I'm sending you to help him in any way you can. And make sure I get the gold I've contracted for."

Eslingen opened his mouth, and closed it again, knowing that protest was futile. He knew exactly what Caiazzo meant by "helping," and he'd be damned before he'd cheat Rathe that way—but to say it outright was to lose his place, with winter coming on and no money saved to tide him over until he found other work. Not that there was much demand for soldiers in Astreiant in the first place, and that brought him back to the dilemma that had kept him here since midsummer.

"Very well," he said. "And what about my usual duties?"

Caiazzo smiled. "I took care of myself long enough, Philip. And Aice can mind the rest."

The magist looked both fond and exasperated at that, but said nothing. Caiazzo folded the note and handed it to Eslingen. "I'm sure Rathe will be glad of your help," he said, with a twist of a smile that wasn't quite a smirk. "But mostly—get the gold."

"Yes, sir," Eslingen said, and turned away.

As MONTEIA HAD predicted, van Duiren returned within the hour to demand Old Steen's effects. Rathe made himself scarce while the Chief Point handed them over, and Lennar, coming to say the coast was clear, reported that the woman had been in a rare temper, though at least she'd had the sense not to turn it on Monteia.

"Because the Chief was a hair's breadth from telling her to get a judge's ruling on the matter," Lennar said. "And that would have spoiled her game."

Rathe nodded, and checked as he saw the figure ahead of him in the station's main room. For a craven instant, he thought about walking away before he got himself in any deeper, but Eslingen was already up to his neck in the matter. There would be no avoiding him, no matter what Monteia said, and he couldn't decide if that thought was pleasant or not.

"Hello, Philip," he said. "I didn't expect you back so soon."

Eslingen looked over his shoulder with a wry smile. "Caiazzo has a claim to make, though I gather we're too late to have the effects impounded."

"Afraid so," Rathe answered. "Not that there was much to consider. As you saw."

"It's the principle of the thing," Eslingen answered, in the dulcet tones that always made Rathe want to snicker. "Lunele—his advocate—is closeted with your Chief, and I imagine she's making that very point."

"I daresay." Rathe lowered his voice slightly, just enough to keep the duty point, all ears at the desk, from hearing clearly. "I don't suppose you'd care to share what Young Steen told you when you took him off? Which I do appreciate, by the way."

"You're welcome," Eslingen answered. "No more than he told you already, I'm afraid. I left him heading for Point of Knives to roust out witnesses to his father's non-marriage."

"Is that where Old Steen lodged?" Rathe asked.

Eslingen shrugged. "So his son says." His gaze sharpened. "And that's important how?"

"Point of Knives—you know the Court of the Thirty-Two Knives, I know I told you about it, and I know Caiazzo has dealings there."

Eslingen gave a soft laugh. "I've had an adventure or two there, yes, since entering his employ. Nothing to concern the points, of course."

"Oh, I'm sure of that," Rathe said, and managed to keep a straight face. The Court of the Thirty-Two Knives had once been a great mansion, fallen into disrepair two centuries ago, and during the civil wars, the original thirty-two knives had turned it into a fortress from which they terrorized most of the area south of the river. It had taken a regiment of soldiers with artillery to batter them into submission, and there were still plenty of folk southriver who would rather handle justice in the Knives' fashion than acknowledge the law or the points. "Point of Knives is the area that grew up around the Court, among other things. The regents forced our surintendant to open a points station there three years ago, but it went to Mirremay, who's a direct descendant of one of the banner-dames—the Knives' only real rivals, and the people who took over when the Knives were driven out. She paid a huge sum in fees to get the place, or so one hears, and she's taking fees hand over fist herself to make up for it. If that's where Old Steen lodged—we won't get any help from Mirremay, not unless Caiazzo's willing to meet her price."

"I don't know that he'd be averse to it," Eslingen said. "Though he does like to get value for money."

"She stays bought," Rathe said, reluctantly. "That's all the good I can say of her."

"Well, if it's just a matter of the fee," Eslingen began, and a door closed sharply upstairs.

Rathe looked up to see Caiazzo's advocate and Monteia emerge from the chief point's workroom, the advocate still talking quietly while Monteia nodded with decreasing patience. The advocate—Lunele—seemed to realize she was harming her case, because she stopped and made a polite curtsy instead, her black-and-red gown rustling. Monteia matched the gesture, and Lunele descended the stairs, as graceful as if she were at a soueraine's ball. She looked discreetly pleased with herself, however, and Rathe's mouth tightened. As Eslingen had just pointed out, Caiazzo was hardly opposed to paying for the law.

"Rathe!" Monteia reached for her pipe, was filling it as she spoke. "A word with you, please."

Rathe looked at Eslingen, who gave a fractional shrug. *And I believe him,* Rathe thought, as he started up the stairs. *Whatever this is about, I don't think Philip knew it beforehand.*

Monteia closed the door of the workroom behind them, and waved Rathe to the nearest stool. She settled herself beside the stove, and lit a long straw to coax her pipe alight. Rathe waited, knowing better than to interrupt, and at last she leaned back in her chair, a cloud of smoke wreathing her head.

"Caiazzo is filing an official complaint," she said, "and making a formal claim against Old Steen's estate. It seems Steen owed him money."

"Right," Rathe said. He didn't believe it for an instant, and from her expression, neither did Monteia. "But why—?" He stopped, shaking his head. "To force an inventory, under judicial supervision. I wonder what he's after?"

"I'm hoping your friend Eslingen can tell us that," Monteia answered.

Rathe paused. "I thought you were warning me off," he said.

Monteia met his gaze squarely. "I was. But Caiazzo's offered us his services, full assistance to the points, and you said it yourself, he proved himself a useful man this past summer."

And Caiazzo's fee'd you. Rathe knew better than to say that aloud, but the knowledge must have shown on his face, because Monteia frowned.

"Yes, there's a fee for it, and a good one. And if you weren't so damned stiff-necked, you'd have a share of it. But you are, and so I don't offer." She held up a hand to forestall his protest. "And there's another reason I accepted. I want this knife where you can keep an eye on him. It's as they say on the caravans: better to invite him in, and have him pissing out of the tent, than the other way around."

There was some truth to that, Rathe thought. It was just—he thought he'd managed to resign himself to the situation. To be thrown into Eslingen's company day and night, working together again—he could hardly expect that they wouldn't fall back into old habits, and he couldn't stop the treacherous eagerness that stole over him at the mere idea. And that was dangerous. Eslingen was still Caiazzo's man, and he couldn't afford to forget it. Even so, he felt his heart lift.

Monteia seemed to have read his thought, and gave a rather sour smile. "Take the rest of the day and sort this out," she said. "I'll have Amarele finish your shift."

"Yes, Chief," Rathe said, and scrambled to obey.

ESLINGEN WAS STILL waiting in the main room, a slightly bemused expression on his face. As Rathe came down the stairs, he came to meet him, saying, "It seems I've been seconded to your service, Adjunct Point."

Beneath the cool drawl, Rathe thought he detected a hint of uncertainty, and it was that he answered. "Yes. And I can't say I'm sorry, either."

The faintest hint of color tinged Eslingen's cheeks. "You know that Caiazzo—"

"Sent you, yes," Rathe interrupted. This was not a discussion he was going to have in the station precincts, or anywhere close at hand. "Betts, I'm out for the rest of the day, Chief's orders. Livsey will take the rest of my shift."

"Right, Adjunct Point," the duty point answered, and did a fair job of hiding her curiosity.

Rathe led the way out of the station and down Carrick Street toward the river, Eslingen following docilely in his wake. He'd thought at first that they could go to Wicked's, but he was too well known there, too much a regular for Eslingen's reappearance not to be remarked, and while he could stand the teasing, he didn't want to have to deal with explanations. He settled instead for a travelers' tavern on the edge of Point of Sighs, and let the waiter talk him into the private cubby he'd wanted in the first place. Eslingen's eyebrows rose, but he slid without complaint into the narrow space. It held no more than the table and a pair of short benches, and the unlit stove beneath the table, and the walls that rose almost to the ceiling were thick oak planks, inlaid with brass disks that guaranteed protection against eavesdroppers.

"How very—intimate, Adjunct Point."

"We need to talk," Rathe said.

Eslingen sobered instantly. "We do. Nico, this was not my idea."

"I didn't think it was," Rathe said. "It's got Caiazzo's handprints all over it."

"True enough. But he's told me off to help you, and I believe he means it."

"Why would he do that?" Rathe demanded. The waiter appeared again, and they broke off to order a pint of wine and a pot of beer for Eslingen, as well as a plate of bread and cheese. When the waiter had bowed himself off, Eslingen shrugged.

"I don't know, except that he doesn't like being cheated."

"Hanse has ways of dealing with that," Rathe said, "and they don't usually involve the points. This had better not be like this summer, him and his gold smuggling."

"Not as far as I know," Eslingen said, but there was the faintest hint of unease in his tone. "And he never had political motives, anyway, you know that."

"No, but it was political, all the same, and Hanse was in it up to his neck."

Eslingen dipped his head in acknowledgement. "True. And I think I can go so far as to say that this business is an attempt to recoup some of the summer's losses. But it's all by way of business, nothing to do with the queen or the succession or anything else political."

Rathe considered him for a long moment. He thought Eslingen was telling the truth, at least as far as he knew it, and it was certainly the case that Caiazzo had never had any real interest in politics. Or, more precisely, not in any one idea or candidate above any other. He was perfectly happy to make money from other people's political ambitions—he was behind half the unlicensed broadsheet printers in the city—but he had none himself. And much of his power would vanish if the laws or the monarch changed too drastically. "Fair enough," he said. "But that still leaves us."

"Yes."

Rathe hadn't expected a direct answer, and leaned back in relief as the waiter returned with their order. After they'd sorted it out and the waiter disappeared again, he said, "Truth is, I wasn't expecting this. I'd—we'd settled things, I thought."

"We had." Eslingen nodded. "I was honest with you before about my situation, Nico, and it hasn't changed. I haven't got the money to leave Caiazzo's service. A month ago, I could maybe have found a place with a company, but I'd have had to leave Astreiant. And now nobody's hiring. I'm trapped worse than I was before."

"And that's my doing," Rathe said.

"No, it's not," Eslingen said. "I could have told you to go drown yourself when you proposed the idea back at midsummer, and I could have hired out any time these last three months. I made my choice, and I'm prepared to stand it. But that's not really the question, is it?"

"So what is the question, then?"

"Caiazzo wants me working with you, and I've no objection to that," Eslingen said. "None whatsoever. I don't much like that Old Steen was killed under my eye. But beyond that—I rather liked the perks of the job, Adjunct Point. I'm hoping to come to some arrangement there as well."

There was color in Eslingen's cheeks despite the insouciant words, and Rathe suspected his own face was pink as well. "If we go on with it, Philip, we'll have to part at the end."

"I know. I didn't say I liked that bit."

Rathe shook his head. "I've done that once already." It had hurt more than he wanted to admit to have to stop seeing the Leaguer, to no longer have him even as a friend. He didn't want to have to learn that absence again.

"This may be all the chance we've got," Eslingen said. "And, who knows, something may come up. I could find another post, or we could fall out, or…."

His voice trailed off as though he'd run out of ideas, and Rathe stared at him. "Or one or both of us could end up dead," he said at last. "I'm not entirely encouraged, Eslingen."

Eslingen grinned. "Well, I don't intend to drive you off, no. Or to get myself killed, for that matter. But—look, when a company goes into quarters, it's common enough to pair off, to take a winter-lover, knowing you'll part at the spring thaws. I promise I don't ask for more than that."

It was tempting, so very tempting. To have Eslingen at his side, in his bed, without having to worry about being seen or having tales get back to the Surintendant of Points…. And Eslingen was right about one thing, they might never get a better chance.

"All right," he said, and held out his hand across the table. Eslingen clasped it, his touch both firm and caressing, and in spite of himself Rathe's breath caught in his throat. He released his hold, swallowing hard, and reached for his glass. "To—what did you call it, winter-lovers?"

"To winter-lovers," Eslingen echoed, and they touched glasses to seal the bargain.

Chapter Three
THE COILS OF THE LAW

ESLINGEN LEANED AGAINST Rathe's very comfortable pillows, smugly aware that he had managed to collect all of them, leaving Rathe braced less than comfortably against the carved bedstead. He was feeling remarkably pleased with himself, and life in general, happily sated for the first time in a month. The open window let in a pleasant breeze, and the ruddy light of the setting sun spilled across the worn floorboards. Rathe stretched, running both hands through his untidy hair, and Eslingen smiled again, watching the play of muscles across his chest and arms.

"Are you hungry?" Rathe asked.

"I couldn't possibly," Eslingen answered, fanning himself, and Rathe shook his head.

"Idiot."

"I suppose we ought to eat," Eslingen said. "But do we have to go out?"

Rathe reached for his shirt, and Eslingen sat up, sighing. Somehow his hair had come loose, and he caught it back again, then reached for his own discarded clothing.

"I could send the weaver's boy down to Wicked's for the ordinary," Rathe offered. "And I've a decent bottle of wine, if you don't mind that instead of beer."

"That sounds lovely," Eslingen answered, and Rathe finished dressing, went down the stairs to find the neighbor's son. Eslingen watched from the window as he crossed the courtyard, a tough, wiry man in a shapeless coat: a common laborer, you would have said, a typical southriver rat, unless you spent the time to talk with him, to tease out the intelligence

35

and humor lurking behind the pointsman's mask. He was more fond of Rathe than he'd ever expected to be, and only hoped he could keep his word at the end of this business. He'd never had a winter-lover he wanted less to leave.

He shoved that thought aside, and turned to light Rathe's candles, glancing around the room as he did. The building had once been a good-sized mansion, fallen into common hands and cut up now into a series of apartments; Rathe's room was large and comfortable, with a generous bed and a sturdy stove and a table and chairs that were clearly second-hand, but clean and well-made. The pointsman certainly didn't spend his coin on clothes, but he didn't stint on other comforts.

The door opened again, and Rathe came back in, a pitcher in one hand. He set it on the washstand for later, and nodded to the candles. "Thanks. Want I should open the wine?"

"Please," Eslingen said, and the simple domesticity of it all clawed at his heart.

The boy appeared with their food before they'd finished the first glass, and they settled to the meal. When only scraps of the berried tart were left, Rathe lit the stove and came back to the table to pour the last of the wine. Eslingen stretched, extending his legs carefully, and Rathe rested both elbows on the table.

"This cargo of Caiazzo's," he said.

Eslingen picked idly at the last of the tart, brittle pastry crusted with sugar. He'd been dreading the question since Caiazzo had come up with this brilliant plan, and still hadn't decided how to answer. "There's only so much I can tell you," he began, and Rathe gave him a rather nasty smile.

"Oh, come on, Philip, you have to trust me sometime."

"No, I don't," Eslingen said automatically.

"Then so much for all those fine words."

"Unfair."

"And I've got two dead men on my books," Rathe said. "What's fair about that?"

"That has nothing to do with Caiazzo's business," Eslingen said. Rathe quirked an eyebrow, and Eslingen sighed. "Not directly, anyway. Look, fair's fair. Promise this won't go toward calling a point—unless it turns out to be part of the murder, which it won't—and I'll tell you what I know."

"You'd trust me that far?" Rathe asked. He sounded almost surprised, and Eslingen shrugged.

"You're trusting me."

"Fair enough."

The silence stretched between them for a long moment, long enough that Eslingen heard the tower clock strike at Point of Sighs, followed by a fainter cascade of chimes from Point of Hearts further up the river.

"That was your cue," Rathe said. "This is where you show me all you know."

"Why, Adjunct Point," Eslingen murmured, and Rathe shook his head, smiling.

"Business before pleasure, damn it."

Eslingen laughed, burying the uncomfortable thought that he was buying Rathe's favor with someone else's secrets. "All right," he said. "If you promise that then—"

"Philip."

"Right." He took a breath, trying to order his thoughts. "Caiazzo's short of ready money," he said. "He'd been funding his caravans out of that gold mine, and when he lost that—he's been struggling and the Old Dame would like very much to find an excuse to put her fingers in the pie. So when Old Steen sent word that he had money to change outside the law—of course he jumped at it."

"Of course," Rathe said.

"I was carrying an offer," Eslingen said. "A legal payment, crowns and pillars, solid coin of the realm, this realm. And no worries for Old Steen about taxes or foreign coin to explain."

"And Caiazzo would have sent it right back out with the caravans," Rathe said appreciatively. "So he wouldn't have to worry about foreign coin, either."

Eslingen nodded. "But that raises the question of who else could afford to take on this much untaxed coin? Dame van Duiren didn't look like any merchant resident—or merchant venturer, for that matter."

"She's somebody's agent," Rathe said. "That's obvious. But, as you say—who needs the trouble of foreign coin?"

Eslingen nodded. Chenedolle's Queen taxed foreign monies, either on its arrival or as it was exchanged or in a half dozen other places as it circulated in her markets. She kept the rate low enough that most people preferred to change their coin legally, and the Queen accumulated foreign coin that only she could spend. There was simply nothing for an ordinary person to gain from trading in it, except for the metal itself. "Goldsmiths? Jewelers? Most of the Silklands coinage is fairly pure."

Rathe stared at him. "Goldsmiths—Astree's tits. Philip, you great lummox, it's the Dis-damned gold again. And that is political, and I will see Caiazzo dance at a rope's end for it."

Eslingen shook his head. "It's not aurichalcum. It's ordinary gold. All right, it was taxed and bound in the Silklands or the League or the islands—maybe even in Chenedolle, some of it—but it was taxed and bound. You can't use it any more than you can use a crown out of your purse. If you had a crown. Can you?"

"I don't know." Rathe calmed as quickly as he'd flared. "It's untaxed. Illicit. That may well give it magistical properties."

"Ask your necromancer," Eslingen said.

"He's not my necromancer," Rathe said. "And anyway, what would a necromancer know about metallurgy? But he probably knows someone who does."

"So we ask him," Eslingen said. "Maybe that'll tell us who's willing to take the chance of crossing Caiazzo. Because that's a risk not many want to run."

Rathe nodded. "I'll do that. And I'll ask some other folk I know what they can tell me about Dame van Duiren. I'll admit to some definite curiosity about that woman." He straightened. "And you, my Philip, can talk to Young Steen. See what he's found for witnesses, help him if you can—he'll trust you, you're Caiazzo's knife."

"I'll do that," Eslingen said, and couldn't repress a grin. "But—surely it can wait till morning?"

"I do keep my promises," Rathe said, with an answering smile. "Come to bed."

POINT OF HOPES was quiet, drowsing in the morning sun, the stack of papers on the duty point's table barely an inch high. Which probably wasn't the only reason for his good mood, Rathe allowed, but it was as good an excuse as any. He had left Eslingen just stirring, and would meet him mid-afternoon to compare notes. In the meantime, he had researches of his own to pursue.

His first order of business was to draft a note to Istre b'Estorr, the University necromancer who had been such a help during the search for the children. As he'd said to Eslingen, it didn't seem likely that b'Estorr would know a great deal about metallurgy himself, but he would certainly know who to ask. He dispatched a runner with the note, and settled to the stack of papers on his desk.

Monteia had left him a copy of the writ left by Caiazzo's advocate, and Rathe read through it with new appreciation for Caiazzo's ability to hire the best. Through his advocate, Caiazzo claimed Old Steen owed him a debt—monies invested in a side venture, nothing to do with Old Steen's ostensible employers, the owners of the ship he captained—and named a sum high enough to entangle everything Old Steen owned. At worst, if the claim was allowed, he could demand that all Old Steen's effects be dragged into the nearest court and valued, and either sold outright to pay the debts, or Dame van Duiren could pay that value to redeem them. A sensible woman would be looking for some deal, and he couldn't help a pang of disappointment. It would be a pity if his new collaboration with Eslingen were to end so quickly.

He tapped on Monteia's door, and pushed it open. "Thanks for giving me the writ copy," he said. "Is she bargaining?"

Monteia looked up from the daybook. "She is not. She denies the debt, and claims it was contracted without her approval as his wife, so it doesn't stand."

Rathe whistled softly. "That's—courageous."

"Or stupid," Monteia said. "Lunele will eat her alive."

Or there was something in Old Steen's effects that van Duiren couldn't afford to let out of her sight. And that something was presumably the location of Old Steen's untaxed gold. Or maybe the gold itself? No, she still had to be searching, or she could simply hand over anything that wasn't relevant, and go collect the gold while Caiazzo sorted through the mess. "And have her advocate for dessert," Rathe said, and was pleased to draw a smile.

"Just so." Monteia frowned at the nib of her pen. "Any luck with your soldier? No, wait, let me rephrase that. Has he been of any help?"

Rathe's cheeks were hot, but he answered steadily. "Some. I've sent him off to talk to Young Steen, on the theory he might hear more honest answers if a pointsman wasn't lurking in the background."

"Makes sense," Monteia said. "In that case, I'd take it kindly if you'd have a word with Dame Lulli. She's mightily distressed by Grandad's death, and you did say you would."

Rathe nodded. It had to be done, and there was nothing more pressing until b'Estorr replied. "I'll do that," he said, and let the door close before Monteia could make any more remarks.

He made his way through the now-bustling streets to Dame Lulli's house. It was hard by Cockerel Row, the street that marked the unofficial boundary of Point of Knives, and he wondered again if Mirremay had her fingers in the business. He wouldn't put it past her, not with the money she'd laid out to get the post—but then, she wasn't stupid, either, and she had to know that the Surintendant of Points was just waiting for her to put a foot wrong. It was probably just that most of the city's criminal business was done in Point of Knives, but he hated coincidences.

Dame Lulli's maid admitted him to the house almost before he'd said his name, and led him into the better of the two front parlors. It was over-decorated, carved paneling warring with old-fashioned tapestries—Oriane and the Sea-bull, the naked goddess with her back turned and one arm draped over the bull's back, the bull nuzzling her happily—and the tall stove was painted with more mythological scenes. In the noon-time warmth, it was unlit, and the half-open window let in a smell of other people's cooking. The maid returned with a pitcher of lemon-water and a plate of small cakes, and a moment later, Dame Lulli made her entrance. She had stopped to change her clothes, or at least to rid herself of a housewife's apron and hood, was neat and prosperous in a russet skirt and bodice, lace showing at neck and sleeves. Eslingen would know the cost to a demming, Rathe thought, and whether it was Guild work or a homelier makeshift; he himself could only note that it was small and delicate and suited the dress.

"Adjunct Point," she said, and settled herself in the carved chair opposite him. "Thank you for making time to see me."

"I'd have come sooner," Rathe said, "except that we've been dealing with a second death as well."

"I'd heard a rumor," Lulli said. "Old Steen killed, too?"

Rathe nodded. "The same night, and probably by the same hand."

Lulli sighed. "I'd hoped it wasn't true. What can I tell you, Adjunct Point?"

"I expect Baiart already asked most of my questions," Rathe said. "But I would take it kindly if you'd go through it with me again."

"Of course," she said, and drew herself up like a noblewoman.

As he'd expected, there wasn't much new to learn. As far as Lulli knew, Grandad had no enemies: he paid his bills on time, he lived quietly in a room behind the kitchen, he didn't even run a tab at the neighborhood tavern.

"Of course, people bought him drinks for the stories," she said. "But when they didn't, if it was quiet, he could pay his own shot." She hesitated. "I don't think all of them were stories, Adjunct Point."

Rathe grinned in spite of himself, thinking of mermaids, and she smiled back.

"Well, no, not those. But I do believe he was a summer-sailor, and I believe he funded that son of his out of what he'd taken."

"You sound as though you had cause to dislike Old Steen," Rathe said.

"Not cause," Lulli said, scrupulously. "No cause at all. But I didn't like him, Adjunct Point. He was a troublemaker, the sly kind—the sort who eggs on another boy to do something bad, and never gets beaten himself. I was always glad when he was at sea." She shook her head. "But Grandad was always happy to see him, foolishly so, I'd have said. If it was just Grandad dead, I'd tell you to check Old Steen's books and see if he'd come into money."

That was something Rathe hadn't considered, though on the face of it, it seemed unlikely. Grandad wasn't the sort to keep a crossbow when he could afford a pistol or a knife. "I don't suppose he owned a crossbow?"

Lulli shook her head. "No. Nothing like that. He had a knife, of course, but that's gone."

She'd been through his things, of course, under Baiart's supervision. "And nothing else was missing?"

"The cap from his head," she began, and someone knocked heavily at the front door.

"Open to the law!"

"What in Heira's name?" Lulli rose to her feet, and Rathe copied her. He heard the maid's footsteps in the hall, and then the sound of the door opening.

"What's the matter—"

"A writ in the Queen's name," a man's voice said. "To seize the property of one Grandad Steen for his heir."

"Oh, no, they don't," Lulli said, grimly, and swept from the parlor.

Rathe followed, one hand on the truncheon beneath his coat. It was a badge of office as well as a weapon; he hoped he would only need the former. The maid was pressed back with the door, and two tall men in leather jerkins had forced their way onto the top step.

"What's the meaning of this?" Lulli demanded, and the foremost man swept his cap on and off again.

"Writ of seizure, dame. You might as well let us in, there's no denying us."

"Let me see that writ," Lulli said, and the leader held it out, but pulled it back when she would have taken it.

"No, no, dame, I'm not letting you rip it up and claim there never was such a paper."

"Don't be ridiculous," Lulli snapped. "Let me see it."

"Let us in first," the leader said, and gave the door another hard shove. The maid squeaked and slid backward on the polished floor, and Rathe decided it had gone far enough.

"What's this, then?"

"No business of yours," the second man rumbled, and the leader gave him an assessing look.

"It's a matter for your mistress, not yourself."

Rathe sighed theatrically, and let his coat fall open. "But a royal writ is very much my business. What's your authority?"

"A royal writ is royal authority," the leader answered, but his voice was fractionally less certain than his words.

"Let me see it," Rathe said. "And don't tell me I'll rip it up."

The leader handed it across, and Rathe scanned the form. As he'd suspected, it was a bailiff's writ, engrossed with several large but unimportant advocate's seals as well as the royal stamp, and he shook his head. "Mind you, I'm tempted, seeing as how this is a bailiff's writ, which is only by a generous stretch a royal document. And it's not a writ of seizure, either. It's a writ of destraint, and it only obliges you, dame, to hold Grandad's possessions until the courts decide who his heir actually is." He handed it back to the leader, keeping his free hand close to his truncheon. It would be a bad fight, bad odds, but he thought he could bluff them back. "Who's your principal? Someone's sent you on a wild goose chase."

"I can't name her, pointsman, you know that," the leader said. He glanced over his shoulder, seemed to read something in the other man's eyes, and took a step back. "Your pardon, dame. But you are required to keep the property intact and inviolate."

"I'd do that for my own honor," Lulli snapped. "And now I'll have the points seal his room, and no one can go in or out until the matter's settled."

"An excellent idea," Rathe said. "That should satisfy your principal."

The leader nodded slowly. "I'll give her that word, then."

"One thing," Rathe said. "What points station signed this?"

The leader hesitated. "Point of Knives."

Rathe sighed. It was no more than he'd expected, but it was one more complication. "Right. You've earned your fee."

The second man peeled himself reluctantly from the door frame, and backed away. The leader followed him, and managed a deliberately too-low bow before he turned away. The maid slammed the door, turning the night locks with trembling hands, and Dame Lulli gathered her into an embrace.

"They're gone," she said. "They're gone and all's well." Her eyes met Rathe's over the girl's head, and he nodded.

"I'll seal the door," he said, "if you have wax I can use. And—just for your own peace of mind—does your knife work days?."

He hadn't wanted to frighten the maid further by being more direct, and was pleased when Lulli nodded. "He will for this."

It was the work of only a few minutes to spread a ragged circle of wax across the shutters and press the head of his truncheon, heavy with the royal seal, into the soft surface. He did the same with the door, covering the lock, but waited until Lulli's watchman arrived before he left. In the street, he squinted at the nearest tower clock—Point of Knives, stubbornly five minutes out of step with the rest of the city—trying to decide if it was too early to meet Eslingen. It was earlier than he'd intended, and he supposed he could talk to Mirremay himself— He allowed himself a crooked grin. No, he was not going to go into Point of Knives without Eslingen at his back.

ESLINGEN PICKED HIS way along the riverfront, past the long low barns that were the rope-walks and the taller warehouses that lined the river's edge. The masts of the ships docked further south along the river's edge rose above the russet-tiled roofs of the warehouses, black needles against the brilliant autumn sky. He threaded his way along the Factors' Walk and crossed onto the docks proper, searching for the flag bearing a woman with a scepter that was the house-mark of the *Soueraine of Bedar-res*. Since joining Caiazzo's service, he'd spent a fair amount of time on the docks, but he hadn't managed to lose the landsman's sense of unease around the river's deep water and swift currents. The high hulls of the ships that carried Astreiant's trade to the edges of the world seemed little protection against the uneasy depths. He told himself it was just reasonable caution, his stars being bad for water, but he couldn't quite rid himself of the sense that the boards were shifting under him as he made his way onto the quay where the *Soueraine* was docked. Laughing gulls wheeled overhead, diving for scraps off the end of the pier; the air smelled of damp and tar and spices and other things he couldn't identify.

The *Soueraine* was smaller than he'd expected, with a sharply raked bow and a pair of the scrolled brass cannon they called chasers tucked up beside the anchor ports. They weren't defensive weapons, and Eslingen gave them a sour glance. He'd had chasers turned on him before, in a fight on the bleak coast north of Altheim, and he hadn't liked it one bit. The *Soueraine* and her captain weren't trying very hard to hide that they were summer-sailors.

He stopped at the base of the gangway, lifting a hand to shade his eyes. "Permission to come aboard?"

For a long moment, there was no answer, but at last a tousled head appeared above the rail. "What's your business?"

"To see Young Steen," Eslingen called back.

"What's the name?"

"Eslingen."

"Come aboard, and I'll see if he's free." The girl vanished.

Eslingen made his way gingerly up the ramp, not at all reassured by the sudden appearance of the little-captain. It growled at him from the rail that guarded the high stern platform, and Eslingen was careful to come no closer. At least the river was relatively quiet here, not as choppy as it could be down by the Exemption Docks. He could hear voices from beneath the deck, quite a few voices, but couldn't make out the words. They didn't sound angry, at least, but it didn't sound precisely like a friendly gathering, either—more like a meeting or the crowd at an auction, though the latter was prohibited shipboard. Cargos were put to bid at the public auction hall in Point of Sighs or in guild-owned halls along Mercandry, where they could be seen and taxed. Not that half those bids weren't fixed in advance, he'd learned that much from Caiazzo, but in theory the system was open and fair.

The voices were suddenly louder, and a door opened between the ladders that led to the stern platform, disgorging a stream of people. There were a good dozen of them—a lunar dozen, Eslingen amended, fifteen, mostly men but a few sharply-dressed women, trailing out from what had to be the captain's cabin. Young Steen trailed behind them, followed by a woman his own age in a well-tailored gown, and one of the other women turned back to take his hand.

"Just say the word, and we'll be there. All the witnesses you need."

"Thank you, Berla. Father would appreciate it." Steen caught Eslingen's eye and nodded, but said nothing until the last of the group was on the gangway, and only the well-dressed woman and the girl remained behind. "Eslingen. What brings you here?"

"I wanted to talk to you about your father's cargo," Eslignen said, with a wary glance at the woman at Steen's shoulder. "I just had a few questions, if you had a moment."

"I'll take my leave, then," the woman said. From the look of her, she was a well-off merchant—or, more likely, a merchant's daughter, Eslingen thought. She looked much of an age with Steen, and women that young didn't own their own combines, worked instead for their mothers and aunts. "But—give it some thought, Steen, will you?"

"I certainly will," Steen said, and bowed over her hand as though he'd been a gentleman. She grinned at that, not at all displeased, and made her way down the gangway.

Steen looked at Eslingen. "Jesine Hardelet," he said. "One of the owners."

"Ah." Eslingen kept his face impassive. That put a different complexion on her visit, and on Steen's graces: she was of an age to be starting a family, and what better way to bind Steen to the family business than to propose he sire a child for her? "And the rest were your witnesses?"

Steen nodded. "Fifteen today, and each of them can bring two or three fellows. Surely that will be enough."

"One would hope," Eslingen said, though, given the look of the group, he rather doubted it. Mostly men, mostly sailors, and none of the women were of a class to stand up to van Duiren's documents. And of course those would be Old Steen's friends and equals, but they wouldn't stand against a signed constract.

"But that's neither here nor there," Steen said. "I've something to tell you, too." He whistled through his teeth and the girl snapped to attention. "Essi, keep the watch. I'm not to be interrupted unless it's serious."

"Yes, captain," the girl answered, and perched on a barrel by the gangway.

"Come within," Young Steen said, and Eslingen followed him into the cabin.

It was bigger than he'd expected, with a front room like a parlor and a door that obviously led to the captain's private quarters. The parlor was dominated by a chart table, and a rack of cubbies was chained to the rear wall. Thick glass sun-stealers caught and magnified the light from the deck above, and a pair of bracket-lanterns were lit as well, the sweet smell of the oil not quite enough to drown out the smell of tar. Steen waved him to a stool, and took another one himself, leaning one elbow on the chart table.

"What did you want with me?" Steen said.

"I came to see if you'd thought of any place your father might have hidden his chest of gold, since it seems clear Dame van Duiren hasn't found it," Eslingen answered. "Or, failing that, where he might have left some key to finding it."

Steen grinned. "Dad was never much for treasure maps."

"And here I thought they were de rigeur," Eslingen said.

"It's not always like the broadsheets," Steen answered. "Dad liked keeping his secrets secret."

Eslingen's heart sank. If Old Steen hadn't kept any record of what he'd done with his treasure, they were beaten before they'd started. Rathe would figure it out, he told himself, and lifted an eyebrow. "Surely he had to take into account the possibility that something might happen to him," he said. "He wouldn't have wanted the gold to be lost entirely."

"You'd think not," Steen answered. "But it would be in his goods if there was anything, and—she's got them. But that's what I wanted to tell you. Jesine—Dame Hardelet—I pointed out van Duiren to her, when we were collecting witnesses, and she said she knows the woman under another name. As far as she knows, Dame Costanze van Duiren is Dame Amielle Delon, and she owns a counting house in Point of Knives. A counting house that employs no clerks, and is almost never open for business, but she pays the rent and keeps stout locks on the doors. What do you say to that?"

"It's interesting," Eslingen agreed. "Very interesting."

"Jesine said she just thought Delon was a fence, there's dozens of them in Point of Knives. But I say she's keeping her real business there." Steen leaned forward. "And I say we should raid the place, see what she's got in her coffers."

"I don't think that's a good idea," Eslingen said.

"Why not? We could be in and out again before she knew what hit her."

"Except she would know," Eslingen said. "Granted, she's probably got more enemies than just you and Caiazzo, but right at the moment, you're the first one she'll point fingers at."

"Then what, we should just do nothing?"

Eslingen shook his head. "Let me tell Rathe, have him put a watch on the place. We might find out more that way than if we just go crashing in without any idea what she uses the place for. Not to mention the points have the rights to break down a door or two if it comes to that."

"You really think he'd do it?" Steen asked.

"He wants to know what's going on," Eslingen said. "He'll do it. I give you my word on it."

Steen nodded slowly. "I'll hold off, then. But if it comes to court without any more than this—I'll have to act, Eslingen."

"Understood," Eslingen answered.

To RATHE'S SURPRISE, Eslingen was more than punctual, arriving at the eating house before the appointed time. The day had turned fair, and they took their meal into the back garden, where the chance of eavesdroppers was diminished. The vines that adorned the brick walls were already turning scarlet, and Rathe eyed them with a certain melancholy. They seemed all too emblematic of this relationship, brilliant and delightful, but all too soon to fade. And that, he told himself, was the worst sort of theatrics—even the crowds at the Bell would scorn such melodrama.

"Any luck?" he asked, and made himself meet Eslingen's eyes with a smile.

Something that might have been worry eased from the other man's face. "Not with what I went to ask," he said. "Apparently Old Steen didn't believe in treasure maps or sharing information. And Young Steen's witnesses are numerous but not what I'd call convincing. But I did find something interesting. His boss knows Dame van Duiren under another name entirely. And she has a counting house that's never seen to do much business, yet somehow still survives."

"That is interesting," Rathe said, once Eslingen had gone through the details. "And I'd guess she's right, your Dame Hardelet—"

"Oh, most definitely not mine," Eslingen said, with a smirk. "She's courting Young Steen, and I think she'll get him."

"Also interesting, but not to the point," Rathe said. "She's probably right, van Duiren's a fence, and that's where she changes her money when she has to."

"So presumably that's where she'll manage this business," Eslingen said. "It stands to reason she won't want anything associated with herself as van Duiren, there's too much chance Caiazzo would find out and tangle all her businesses in the courts. What do you want to wager that she's got Old Steen's papers there?"

"It's possible," Rathe said.

"So maybe we should make sure," Eslingen said. "Sneak in, take a quick look round—"

Rathe shook his head. "Not yet," he said. "Once we do that, she'll know we've found the place. She's bound to have wards on the place, magistical and not, and—well, I'm good, but I'm not good enough to be sure I can reset them perfectly."

"What about b'Estorr?" Eslingen asked.

"He's a necromancer, Philip. He doesn't do locks." Rathe paused. "Not as far as I know, anyway. And even the best lockpicks leave signs. How do you think we call half our points?"

Eslingen lifted a hand, acknowledging the point like a fencer admitting a hit. "And here I thought you'd have an expert ready to hand."

"Sadly, no." Rathe drained the last of his wine. "Though if it comes to that, there are tools—but no matter. We'll put a watch on the place, certainly. One of the apprentices, maybe, or a junior, someone van Duiren's unlikely to have noticed. That should give us an idea if she's using it for this business. In the meantime, though—we do need to talk to Istre."

"I thought you said he didn't do locks," Eslingen said, and fished in his purse for the money for his meal.

"He doesn't." Rathe tossed his share of the reckoning onto the table. "But he does understand about gold, and what he doesn't know—he'll know who we should ask."

"Are you back on that again?" Eslingen demanded. "I tell you, Caiazzo's not interested in politics. The government suits him just fine the way it is."

"And I believe you," Rathe answered, though a part of him wasn't entirely sure. "But I'm going to have to answer to the Surintendant sooner or later, and I want to rule out politics before then."

They made their way across Temple Bridge toward the Pantheon and Temple Fair, Eslingen lagging only a little behind as they passed along the row of printers' shops on the east side of the square. Checking the broadsheet horoscopes, Rathe knew, and kept his own gaze turned resolutely away. The last thing he needed was to be distracted by unlicensed printers, and particularly not ones printing under Caiazzo's coin. They passed through the Northgate and made their way into the University grounds. The winter term was well begun, and the streets were crowded with students in their short gray gowns, worn open over every possible combination of fashion. That was against University rules, Rathe knew, and he wasn't surprised to see various of them pause at the doorways of the lecture halls to do up a minimum number of buttons before rushing inside.

b'Estorr, like most of the senior masters, had his lodgings on the University grounds. Rathe led them across the open courtyard, scattering a flock of gargoyles scrabbling at a pile of gardeners' waste, and knocked at the porter's door. He expected b'Estorr to be at classes, but to his surprise, the porter said he was in, and a few moments later the necromancer himself appeared at the top of the stairs to beckon them up. His rooms were comfortable, parlor and bedroom and study as well as the necessary, but, as always, Rathe felt a faint chill at the back of his neck as he came through the door. No natural chill, that, not on a warm autumn day, but the presence of b'Estorr's personal ghosts, gathered during his service with the late king of Chadron. Out of the corner of his eye, he saw Eslingen's eyebrow wing upward as he felt the same touch, and hoped the Leaguer wouldn't say anything inappropriate.

If b'Estorr saw, he ignored it, and waved them toward the chairs that stood beside the unlit stove. "I've just had tea brought up," he said. "It should still be hot enough."

Eslingen shook his head, but Rathe accepted the offer, settled into the more comfortable of the two chairs b'Estorr kept for visitors. b'Estorr poured himself a cup as well, and looked quizzically from one to the other.

"What brings both of you to me?" he asked, and Rathe thought there was a distinctly wary note in his voice. "I didn't think you were allowed to work in harness these days."

"Is it that obvious?" Rathe asked, and b'Estorr nodded. Eslingen looked faintly abashed, and brushed at his hair as though an insect had landed there. b'Estorr frowned, seeing that, and made a small gesture with his left hand. The chill faded, almost reluctantly, and Rathe knew the ghosts had been warned to stand further off. From Eslingen's unhappy look, he knew it, too, but Rathe pretended he hadn't seen.

"Anything that makes Hanselin Caiazzo join forces with the points and requires my attention...." b'Estorr let his voice trail off. "Let's just say it makes me nervous, especially after this summer."

"And there's an unholy echo of this summer in the business," Rathe said, "which I'd like to rule out as quickly as possible. In confidence, Istre—"

"My word on it," b'Estorr said quickly.

"—there's a chest of gold missing, gold that's never been taxed, and two dead men into the bargain."

"So far," Eslingen said.

"There's a cheery thought," Rathe said. "Yeah, so far. And I'm wondering—I know that aurichalcum, queen's gold, it's magistically pure, and so it has power. That's why the queen keeps possession of it herself, or doles it out to trusted associates."

"Well," b'Estorr began, and stopped at Rathe's look. "Well, yes. That's the theory."

"I know there's a certain amount of license given to the University, and I know there's some queen's gold circulating illegally," Rathe said. "That's not what I'm interested in. This missing gold, being untaxed—I wondered whether it had any similar properties?"

"Now there's an interesting question," b'Estorr said. "Technically—well, no, that's not really true. All coin is bound to the realm by the design on its face, Chenedolle's coin to Chenedolle, Chadron's to Chadron, the League's to their individual cities, and so on. Foreign coin ought to be inherently somewhat unstable, and I assume that the tax and the tax mark is intended to bind it somehow, but I don't really know. I don't generally use royal metals in my work."

"Who does, then?" Rathe asked. "And who can tell me about the taxes?"

"You want one of the Fellows," b'Estorr said. "The Royal Fellows. They're in charge of metallurgy and related arts. And of all of them—Caillavet Vair is your best bet."

"All right," Rathe said, doubtfully, and b'Estorr smiled.

"You'll like her, Nico. She's very like you."

Chapter Four
THE ROYAL METAL

VAIR DID NOT live in the University precinct, but further north, where the city's buildings thinned out to make room for larger houses. It was a long walk, outside the usual range of the city's low-flyers, but a pleasant one, the afternoon sun dipping into the west, the waning light gilding the dusty streets. The trees were changing here, too, green giving way to gold and russet-brown, and as they made their way into the wealthier neighborhoods, where the minor nobility mingled with the most successful merchants, the air had the heady smell of turned loam and the whiff of burning leaves. Rathe opened the front of his jerkin, enjoying the warmth, and saw that Eslingen was smiling.

"What?" Rathe asked.

Eslingen tipped his head to one side. The brim of his hat shaded his face, but couldn't hide the mischief in his expression. "You know, this Mistress Vair—she doesn't know we're coming."

"She does," Rathe said. He knew where this was going. "Istre sent a runner."

"Yes, but she doesn't know when we'll get there." Eslingen nodded to their right, where a painted banner stirred in the lazy breeze. It marked the entrance to a wine bower, one of the garden establishments that flourished through the long summer. There would be musicians and dancing in the evenings, and the clock round there were private rooms, screened by curtains of flowering vines. Rathe shook his head.

"No," he said. "Business first."

Eslingen laughed. "What about after?"

"After?" Rathe grinned. "As long as you're paying. I'm a poor pointsman, Philip. You're in private service."

"I'd count it coin well spent," Eslingen answered, not quite lightly enough, and Rathe looked away. That was the skeleton at the feast, the certain knowledge that they'd have to part when the job was over. And maybe we won't, he thought. As long as we're discreet, as long as we're careful not to mix our respective businesses—but even if they could manage it, no one would believe he was unaffected. Caiazzo could fee a pointsman with other things than coin. Maybe he could persuade Eslingen to leave Caiazzo's service, could loan him the coin to keep him over the winter—better still, let him stay the winter, there was room enough, though there was no telling if Eslingen would be willing to accept that great a favor. Or if it would be wise—they might not suit that well, after all, and then where would they be?

Rathe shook the thought away, and managed a quick smile. "It's your money, Lieutenant."

Vair's house lay just at the edge of the suburbs, where the houses were separated by fields where cattle grazed, and they had to step from the road to make way for an ox-drawn wain piled high with hay. It was a long, low building that looked as though it might have been a barn or a threshing house before the city came to meet it—perhaps belonging to the stone house a little further up the road, it had the look of a manor. It was not the sort of place Rathe would have expected to find a Royal Fellow—they generally lived in more state than this—but perhaps Vair needed space for a workshop. The girl who answered the door admitted that Maseigne was at home, and led them into a sun-washed parlor. The room was nicely furnished, a pleasant mix of old and new, but the floors were bare stone.

"Maseigne," Eslingen murmured. "Do you think she deserves the title?"

Rathe glanced around the room again, gauging the quality of the furniture. There was a crest carved into the back of one tall chair, though he didn't recognize the design, and same crest appeared on a set of silver-bound faience plates that stood in a tall cabinet. "I'm beginning to think she might."

The maidservant reappeared, and dropped the barest of curtsies. "Maseigne will see you. If you'll come with me?"

"Of course," Rathe said.

She led them down a short hall that ran the width of the narrow house, and emerged into an old-fashioned solar, its long windows looking out into a walled formal garden, its late-blooming flowers severely confined to stone-walled beds. It was a style Rathe had never much favored, but it fitted with the antique feeling of the house. Vair herself sat in a patch of sun between the windows, her back to them and her face in shadow.

"The pointsmen, Maseigne," the girl announced, and withdrew, closing the door gently behind her.

Rathe bowed, aware that Eslingen's gesture was more elegant, and came on into the room. Now he could see why the floors were bare, and why the garden was so formally tended: Caillavet Vair sat in a wheeled chair, the skirts of her gray gown folded around her like a blanket. Her hands were free of both rings and paint, but the Fellows' collar across her shoulders was jewel enough.

"Adjunct Point Rathe and Lieutenant Eslingen," she said. "Istre b'Estorr says I should assist you."

Her tone was neutral, if anything merely idly curious, and Rathe gave her a sharp look. It was never wise to underestimate any member of the University, and she was clearly no exception.

"That's right," he said. "I—we—are looking for information about the royal metals and how they work. Gold in particular."

"I would have thought you'd learned all you needed to know about that this summer," she said, with a fleeting smile. "Please, be seated." She waved to the tambours that stood against the wall.

"Thank you, Maseigne," Eslingen murmured, and pulled two of them closer to her chair.

"I know more than I did about aurichalcum," Rathe said, "but not much at all about ordinary gold, at least not in a magistical sense. Whether it can be used in the same ways as aurichalcum, for example."

Vair tipped her head to one side. Her hair was confined by a lace cap and a strand of pearls, with a single larger pearl at the center parting of her hair. "I could spend most of the afternoon sharing a great deal of interesting but possibly irrelevant information, or you could tell me what you really need to know."

Rathe hesitated. The last thing he wanted was to rouse suspicions about Caiazzo among the Royal Fellows, but he didn't see that he had a choice. "All right, Maseigne," he said. "But there's a good chance I might miss the right question, not knowing enough about the subject."

Vair smiled. "I expect we can resolve that, Adjunct Point, if and when the problem should arise."

"All right," Rathe said again. "As I said, it's about gold—a chest of gold smuggled ashore, we think, by a summer-sailor. The chest has gone missing, and there are several interested parties, but my immediate concern is whether foreign gold, untaxed gold, has any special value to a magist."

Vair grinned. "That's a much disputed question. Ask any five Fellows, and you'll get seven answers." She sobered instantly. "But forgive me. I'm sure that if Istre sent you to me, it's not a matter for academic jokes."

"Sadly, no," Rathe said. "I've two dead men on my books already."

Vair dipped her head in acknowledgement. "And that, indeed, is nothing to mock." She folded her long hands, resting her elbows on the arms of her chair. "Does untaxed foreign gold have magistical effect? My answer wasn't entirely a joke, unfortunately. Traditionally, foreign gold, which by definition isn't taxed by our Queen, has been used in certain magistical operations. It's not nearly as powerful as aurichalcum, for which I'm sure we're all grateful."

Out of the corner of his eye, Rathe saw Eslingen's mouth curl up into a rueful smile. They'd both seen and felt the effects of aurichalcum during the hunt for the children, when an orrery of the pure metal had set all the city's clocks out of tune; felt it, too, when the orrery was destroyed, its power annilhilating its maker as though the man had never existed.

Vair said, "In recent years—since before the current Queen's reign, in fact—most magists have believed that the binding implicit in the minting of a coin was enough to dilute its potency beyond practical use, and that the tax mark placed on duly received coin was magistically unnecessary. However, the tax revenues involved are sufficient that there seemed to be no real need to meddle with the system. But because the concern has been more fiscal than otherwise, there's not been much interest in making sure that nothing slips through the cracks. A few untaxed, unstamped coins here and there simply didn't seem to matter—they weren't a danger, and the revenue their tax would bring in wouldn't pay for the effort to find them."

"But?" Rathe said, and she gave a thin smile.

"But. There has been a rise in certain magistical—let's not call them crimes, they're not precisely that. Activities, perhaps. Certain magistical activities that are best accomplished with aurichalcum or a near similitude, and some of us have begun to consider that untaxed gold may not be as harmless as we thought. And as Her Majesty has not yet named an heir…." Vair shrugged.

And that brought it back to politics again. Rathe swallowed a curse. Succession politics had begun the matter of the stolen children, though a madman had tried to turn it to his own ends. The succession was what had the court on edge and city's Regents minding their purse strings and the Surintendant eyeing every common crime for some hint of political intent.

"Our simplest defense against this has been that it takes a considerable quantity of untaxed gold to have any serious effect," Vair said. "The Queen's tax collectors generally take care of that for us. But now you tell me that an entire chest of gold—foreign, untaxed gold—is up for sale in Astreiant. I can't say I find this calming, Adjunct Point."

"No more do I," Rathe answered. "Still—politics isn't my business, maseigne, but I don't see what a southriver merchant who's probably a fence can have to do with the succession."

"Unless she's acting as agent for someone," Vair said.

"I've seen no sign of it," Rathe said, "though I'll look into it now, be sure of that."

"And there is also Master Caiazzo to consider," Vair said.

Eslingen stirred. "Who would not have sent me to cooperate with the points if he were playing politics, maseigne."

"Most likely not." Vair nodded. "But I can't discount the possibility."

"Everything that I've seen so far points to this being about the coin as coin," Rathe said slowly. "But if it is political—where would you suggest we look?"

Vair hesitated. "We—the Fellows—have heard certain rumors within the University, that certain factions might have some hand in politics, some candidate to support. But we have no proof."

Rathe looked at her. "I don't suppose you could give me a better hint than that?"

She hesitated again, but shook her head with what looked like genuine regret. "I'm sorry, Adjunct Point. The situation is too delicate to mention names, even under these circumstances. But if you should find anything that points back to the University, or toward any magist in particular…."

Rathe sighed. "Be sure I'll consult you," he said, and she nodded.

"It would be very helpful."

THEY MADE THEIR way back toward town in thoughtful silence. The breeze had picked up, as it often did toward evening, blowing dust and strands of hay across the road, while in a field between two houses a pair of young bay horses chased leaves and each other across their paddock. Eslingen gave them an appraising glance, regretting again the rangy chestnut he'd sold at the beginning of the summer, but there was no possibility that he could afford to keep a horse in the city. Nor would Caiazzo stand for it. The merchant-venturer kept no stable of his own, and

Eslingen had never known him to do more than borrow a horse from one of his caravaners. Still, those were pretty creatures, and he glanced back in spite of himself, until the turn of the road cut off his view.

"This doesn't make things any better," Rathe muttered, and Eslingen shook himself.

"More politics, you mean? No, it doesn't."

"And the University," Rathe said. "I'm sure Istre will help, but—we've never had much luck asserting our authority over the Three Nations, never mind their masters."

The Three Nations were the students, Eslingen knew, who were notorious for what he felt was a distinctly unscholarly tendency to drop their books and draw knives over the most unlikely quarrels. He said, "Do you think she's right?"

"That there is some sort of political conspiracy within the University?" Rathe shrugged. "I wouldn't bet against it."

He was looking uncommonly discouraged, Eslingen thought, not like him at all. They had almost reached the wine bower, its banner rippling in the breeze, and he touched Rathe's shoulder. "I promised you an early supper," he said.

"And a bit more besides," Rathe said, but the words sounded forced.

"Food and a decent bottle of wine to start," Eslingen said, "and a private place to talk. For the rest—we'll see."

The bower was uncrowded at this hour, the midday crowd long past, the evening not yet begun, and Eslingen turned his best smile on the young hostess. She agreed to rent them a private table and to serve up a pint of the pale Silklands wine that was Rathe's current favorite along with a plate of bread and cheese to stay their appetite until the evening's ordinary was ready. They were led toward the rear of the bower, across the central garden where the grass had been trampled almost to bare ground by the summer's hard use. The private tables were set up within small tents of brightly painted canvas, divided from each other by hedges of thorny rose; there were small braziers in each one now, and lanterns hanging from the center posts, but at the moment the sun on the canvas kept them warm enough. The chairs were piled with cushions—enough, Esingen noted, to make quite a comfortable bed on the grass between the table and the tent's rear wall—and the air smelled of late roses and the oil in the lamps. The waiter fetched their order, and offered with a leer to close the curtains, but Eslingen shook his head.

"Later," he said, and the waiter withdrew.

"You'll ruin your reputation," Rathe said, and poured the wine.

Eslingen stretched his feet out under the table, and leaned back in his chair. "Or yours."

"That's done already," Rathe said, with a grin. "Damn it. You're sure Caiazzo's not playing politics?"

"As sure as I can be," Eslingen said. "I've seen no signs of it, I know what he does need gold for, and—as I said, it just doesn't pay."

Rathe nodded. "And there's Mirremay to think about."

"What about her?" Eslingen lifted his wine in salute.

"That's right, I haven't told you." Quickly, Rathe sketched out his encounter with the enforcement men at Dame Lulli's. "And Mirremay signed the writ. I hadn't really had her on my books, but now—now I think I have to consider her."

"From what you've said, I don't see how she's involved in politics," Eslingen said.

"I'm not sure I do, either," Rathe said, frankly. "It's just that—I know she spent a lot of money to buy her post, and to get the Regents on her side, because the Surintendant didn't want to give her Point of Knives in the first place."

"She's that bad?"

"She's the direct descendant of the Bannerdames," Rathe said. "Not that they were bannerdames, they were a pack of bandits who took over part of Point of Knives after the Court was destroyed."

"What a charming and peaceful city this is," Eslingen said.

Rathe looked torn between pride and guilt. "I never said there weren't interesting people southriver."

"I do see why your boss might not want her in charge," Eslingen said.

Rathe nodded. "Her great-grandmother was one of the worst of them, and don't think she's forgotten."

"Lovely," Eslingen said.

"Yeah." Rathe leaned back as the waiter appeared with the first course of the night's ordinary, a pale soup smelling of cinnamon and winter gourds. When their bowls had been filled and the waiter had disappeared again, Rathe sighed. "I need to have a word with Mirremay, I suppose, which is a bit—ticklish—at the best of times. I'm Point of Hopes, not Knives. She's not actually a chief point, just a head point, which may not seem like much of a difference to you, but—"

"Oh, believe me, I'm very sensitive to all the little nuances of degree," Eslingen said. "I've served with sixteen-quarter nobles who wouldn't sit down at table with common folk under the rank of colonel, and that when the 'table' was the tail of a wagon balanced on a pair of powder kegs."

"Mirremay's worse," Rathe said.

"I'll refrain from making the obvious remark," Eslingen said, and was pleased to draw a smile.

"What, that common folk are worse about such titles as they've earned?"

"I'd never suggest such a thing," Eslingen said.

"I don't like it that she's signing bailiff's writs on van Duiren's account," Rathe said. "That—well, I'm sure she was well fee'd for it, but it smacks of politics. And I don't trust her."

"Why not?" Eslingen paused, but there was no good way to say it. "Plenty of the points take fees, and are still good for their word."

"My own chief among them," Rathe said. "Yes, I know. And Mirremay stays bought, or always has. It's just—she's too much like her great-grandmother for my comfort, that's all."

And are you like your great-grandmother? Eslingen wondered. He himself had never known his mother, had been left to his father's raising and the streets and horse barns of Esling, and left there as soon as he was old enough to beg a place in one of the mercenary companies that passed through the city. But Rathe was southriver born and bred, a child of Astreiant, and Eslingen knew nothing at all of the man's family. He opened his mouth to ask, then closed it again, unaccountably shy. He could still hear Rathe's pronouncement on Old Steen, *a motherless man but no worse than many,* and though he'd heard worse, he had no real desire to see even pity in Rathe's eyes. He didn't know Rathe's stars, either, not even his solar sign, but that was a question even more intimate, and he reached for the wine instead, refilling their glasses.

"The thing is, I can't see how Mirremay would use the coin," Rathe said. "If she had it, I mean. Yes, she spent a huge sum to buy the post, but this is gold she can't use."

"Could she change it through a fence?" Eslingen asked. "Or in the Court of the Thirty-Two Knives?"

Rathe shook his head. "I don't see how. Not so much of it, not at anything close to its worth."

"And Caiazzo can use it on the caravan roads at near its value," Eslingen said. "But Mirremay—presumably she doesn't have any foreign ventures?"

"Not that I know of," Rathe said, "and I think I'd've heard. And that leaves politics." He shook his head. "I'll have to talk to her, but I can't say I'm looking forward to it."

"I assume you mean 'we' have to talk to her," Eslingen said.

"Oh, yes," Rathe said. "I'm not going into Point of Knives on my own."

One of the bower's younger servants arrived then with a basket of kindling and a taper, and Eslingen nodded for him to build up the fire in the brazier. He ordered another pint of wine as well, and looked at Rathe.

"Of course I'll come with you, and if your sanction extends so far, I'll even go armed."

Rathe nodded.

"In the meantime, though—" Eslingen gestured to the tent's painted walls. Outside, the crowd had grown, and a pair of fiddlers was tuning, ready to start the dancing as the great sun set. "There's nothing we can do about it tonight. Let's enjoy what we have."

For a moment, he thought Rathe was going to refuse, but then the pointsman reached for his wine. "You're right. We should enjoy this—"

He bit off the rest of his words, but Eslingen knew perfectly well what they would have been: *we should enjoy this while we can.* And that, at least, was something he knew how to manage. He set himself to be at his most charming, light gossip and jokes without bite that had Rathe rolling his eyes even as he grinned.

He kept up the nonsense through the two removes of the meal, feeling Rathe's mood ease and rise, and when there was nothing left but crumb from the gingercakes, he reached for Rathe's hand, turning it to kiss the callused palm as though he were in fact the gentleman he pretended.

Rathe caught him by the chin instead, pulling his head up to fix him with an almost angry stare. "Don't play-act."

Eslingen blinked, startled, but answered with reflexive honestly. "I'm not. I don't, not—" *Not when it matters,* he had been going to say, but— that was not a thing said between winter-lovers. "Not now," he finished, and wasn't sure that wasn't worse.

Rathe glared at him, the gray eyes narrowed, and Eslingen leaned in to kiss him, hard and fierce. There was an instant's pause, and then Rathe responded just as fiercely, pushing him back in turn. Eslingen gave way willingly, thinking of the piles of pillows, but when he broke the kiss to reach for the nearest, Rathe pulled back, shaking his head.

"Let's go home," he said.

THERE WAS NO point in going into Point of Knives before ten o'clock—
by then, the night workers and knives would be well abed, and the first
flurry of business would be concluded—and Rathe allowed himself the
indulgence of sleeping in. When he woke, well past sunrise, the other
half of the bed was empty, and he was startled and a little annoyed to
feel momentarily bereft. He shoved that thought away and built up the
fire, then went downstairs to the well to fetch the morning's water, trying
not to wonder where Eslingen had gone. Probably to fetch clean linen,
he told himself, or a longer blade than was legal in the city—though the
more he thought about it, the less it seemed like a good idea to go into
Point of Knives carrying weapons that were conspicuously in violation
of the law.

He had just finished shaving when the door opened and Eslingen appeared, a basket tucked under one arm. "Oh, you're awake," he said, and
set the basket on the table. "I brought breakfast."

"Thanks."

Eslingen began unloading the basket, setting out bread and honeyed
cheese and a crock of salt butter. Rathe moved the kettle to the front
of the stove, savoring the sheer ordinariness of the moment. Eslingen
finished arranging his purchases—he was surprisingly finicky in some
things, Rathe noted—and pulled out the rolled cylinder of paper he'd
tucked into a corner of the basket. Rathe lifted an eyebrow, recognizing a
vice familiar from the summer.

"Broadsheet prophecies? The printers have them out already?"

"The early printer catches my demming," Eslingen answered. "At least
today. I'd have brought you one, but I don't know your stars."

"No more you do," Rathe said, the words suddenly tight in his throat.
He made himself go on making the tea, spooning the dry leaves into the
pot. The kettle had begun to hiss, and he poured the water with extra
care, brought the pot to the table to steep.

"I'm not asking," Eslingen said. He did a creditable job of not sounding
hurt, but there was a bleak look in his eyes. "You'd be a fool to tell me, me
being Caiazzo's man."

And so he would. Rathe knew it perfectly well—he'd kept his natal
horoscope a secret since his apprentice days, when he'd seen an entire
glassblower's workshop poisoned through the similarity of their stars—
and Hanselin Caiazzo was the last man he'd want to trust with anything
that could be turned against him. Still, most people were willing to share
their solar signs, there wasn't much even a skilled astrologer or magist
could do with that. And yet— He forced a smile.

"The Pillars of Justice are well aspected in my horoscope," he offered, and Eslingen snorted, as though it were only a joke.

"That shocks me to the core, Adjunct Point." He flattened his sheet of paper, not bothering to hide the symbol at the top—the Horse, Rathe noted, in spite of himself, and felt a pang of guilt. The tea was ready; he poured them each a cup and cut himself a slice of bread. They ate in silence, not precisely uncomfortable, and then Eslingen laughed and picked up the broadsheet again.

""Stallions quarrel in a field,'" he read, "'but do no harm.'"

Rathe blinked, then shook his head. "Do you think this counts, or do we have something more to look forward to?"

"I'd like to think this was it," Eslingen said, "but from everything you said about this Mirremay...."

"Yeah," Rathe said. "Somehow I doubt it." The tower clock at the end of the Leathersellers' Hall struck the half hour, and he allowed himself a sigh. "And it's time to be getting on with it."

"Lovely," Eslingen said, but tidied the remains of breakfast back into the basket. Rathe swallowed the last of his tea, and crossed to the pegs by the door to collect his truncheon and leather jerkin. It wasn't often he needed to wear both, but he wanted the protection both of his badge of office and leather cured hard enough to turn a blade. He turned, still tugging the last laces home, to see Eslingen settling his coat onto his shoulders. It was second-hand, made over to fit, but it took a careful eye to see where the cuts had been made. A line of braid covered where the hem had been let down, blue-black on indigo, and the buttons and the fittings of the belt that held his knife were at least false silver. And, Rathe noted, the knife itself was a good two inches longer than the city's legal limit. Eslingen saw where he was looking, and shrugged.

"Surely you'll stand bond for me, under the circumstances?"

"I suppose I'll have to," Rathe answered. He slipped his own knife onto his belt—the legal length and no more—and worked his shoulders to settle the jerkin more comfortably. "I'm not planning to cause trouble," he said.

"No more am I," Eslingen answered promptly. "But I believe in being prepared."

"Right," Rathe said, with a certain amount of skepticism, and started down the stairs.

They followed Customs Road east towards Jascinte's Well, where the territories of Hopes, Sighs, and Knives all met. Rathe paused at the fountain in the center of the open square to draw himself a cup of water, and let his gaze sweep across the broad space. Things seemed quiet enough, the pens between the two wings of the Drovers' Hall empty except for a sleeping dog and a gargoyle scrabbling in the near-empty mangers, the shops unshuttered and ready for business, though only a few women were moving in the street, baskets over their arms. Eslingen took the cup and drank as well, leaning close to slacken the chain that pinned the cup to the carved stone.

"Just how much trouble are you expecting?" he asked quietly.

"I don't know," Rathe admitted. "It all depends on Mirremay."

Eslingen gave him a look, and set the cup back in its niche. "I could wish you were a bit more certain, Adjunct Point."

"If it all goes wrong, I'm counting on you to run for help," Rathe said.

"Yes, but to whom?" Eslingen unobtrusively loosened his knife in its sheath.

That was an excellent question, Rathe admitted. Properly speaking, the answer should be the nearest points station, which would be Point of Sighs, but practically speaking that would involve complicated explanations and might take time they wouldn't have. "I can't believe I'm saying this, but—Caiazzo, he'd be the fastest."

Eslingen nodded. "And he has a few connections in the area."

Rathe winced. It was all too easy to imagine the riot that would result. "I'm really hoping to get out of this without any fighting."

"I hope you can," Eslingen said, doubtfully, and Rathe sighed.

"Let's go."

He led the way through the narrowing maze of streets toward the armory that had been converted to the station at Point of Knives. This was the first part of Astreiant built outside the walls, on the south bank of the Sier away from the safe, respectable parts of the city. The first theaters had been here, but quickly moved to Point of Dreams; it had also been home to the first merchant-venturers, and the buildings still bore the stamp of the caravan-trade, built low and long around narrow inner courts where goods could be kept until they were carried across the river. There had been windmills, too, though that trade had moved still further east into Customs Point, where there were fewer buildings to block the onshore winds.

Rumor had it that Mirremay had spent a fair amount of her own coin turning the old building into something more like a regular points station, and certainly there seemed to be new wood and brick on every part of the façade. The clock tower, too, was new, built into an afterthought of a gable, and Rathe gave it all an unhappy glance. If Mirremay had paid for most of this herself, it was another reason she'd be in need of coin.

The main door was closed, and Rathe frowned. That was against general policy, though if Mirremay had upset the population that far—but, no, there was an inner door, and it stood partly open. Rathe tugged the bell rope anyway, listening for the bell's distant clatter, but before he could push the inner door back, Eslingen spoke at his shoulder.

"Nico."

Rathe glanced over his shoulder, and swallowed a curse. Three men and a woman were converging on them, and the street was suddenly empty, barren of witnesses and help alike. He took a step away from the door, not wanting to be caught against the station wall, and saw Eslingen do the same. The strangers carried pointsmen's truncheons, and the woman wore her jerkin open over a neat russet skirt and bodice, but Rathe couldn't see them as friendly.

"What station, friend?" the woman asked, and pointed to Rathe's hip with her drawn truncheon.

"Point of Hopes," Rathe answered. "I was hoping for a word with the Head Point."

The title was a mistake, he knew it as soon as the words were out of his mouth, and the biggest of the men scowled.

"Don't know why the chief would want to see you. And who's he?"

Eslingen spread his hands slowly, showing them empty, but at the same time clearing the skirts of his coat in case he had to draw his knife. "My name's Eslingen."

"Client?" the woman said, to Rathe, who shook his head.

"He's working with me on a problem we're having. And I was hoping the chief might be able to help us out."

"That sort of request ought to be made properly," the woman said. "In writing."

"The matter's urgent—" Rathe began.

"It's not respectful," the big man said.

Rathe swallowed a curse. "There's no disrespect meant," he said. "I'd just like to have a word with Mirremay."

"Chief Point Mirremay." That was another of the men, fair-haired and wiry, and Rathe dipped his head in acknowledgement.

"Chief Point Mirremay," he said.

"I don't believe she wants to see you," the woman said. "Send a proper request, pointsman, and we'll see." She waved her hand toward the street. "That's your way."

"I don't want to make trouble," Rathe said, "but, as I said, the matter's urgent. I don't have time to send a request and have it sent back five times on points of procedure. And it's Adjunct Point. If we're talking titles."

The big man snarled and took a step forward, but the woman lifted a hand. Eslingen froze, his hand not quite reaching for his knife, and Rathe slid his own hand toward his truncheon. Behind them, a woman laughed.

"Chaudet, you overstep. Our colleagues are always welcome in Point of Knives. Particularly Adjunct Point Rathe."

Rathe turned, slowly, not wanting to take too much attention away from the group in the street. "Chief Point Mirremay."

"Head Point," she corrected, with a smile. She was small, with a ripe figure, and knowing eyes in a heart-shaped face. "And of course you're welcome, you and the lieutenant. Come inside, and tell me how I can be of service."

Rathe looked at Eslingen, seeing the same reluctance in the Leaguer's face. To walk into what could very easily become a trap—but surely Mirremay had more sense than to attack her colleagues. He, at least, would be missed, be looked for, though not as quickly as he would be if he were on regular duty; it was a serious risk, even for an entire chest of gold. He hoped to hell Eslingen's horoscope would cover both of them.

"Thank you," he said, and Mirremay took a step back, pulling the door fully open. Rathe stepped through, aware of Chaudet's eyes on his back, and hoped they weren't making a serious mistake.

MIRREMAY'S WORKROOM WAS unexpectedly pleasant, with glass in the windows and a painted stove in one corner. Her broad table was piled high with ledgers and case books and random drifts of paper; there was a stool at one end, ready for a secretary to take dictation, but the secretary herself was nowhere in sight. Mirremay leaned her hip against the table's edge, not bothering to ask them to sit.

"So, Rathe," she said. "What brings you here, with your black dog at your heels?"

Rathe saw Eslingen's eyebrows rise at that, but kept his own expression neutral. "Two murders, Chief Point." *As you very well know.* This time, she did not correct him.

"That's your business in Point of Hopes," Mirremay said promptly. "Monteia's made that quite clear."

"And yet it was your seal on a bailiff's writ I handled just yesterday," Rathe said.

"Ah, but that is my business," Mirremay said. She was enjoying this entirely too much, Rathe thought. "The lady resides in Point of Knives, and her legal recourse is my responsibility."

"Even when her title to those goods is very much in question?" Rathe tipped his head to one side.

"That's a matter for the courts, not me."

"And when the bailiff's men come bullying honest householders," Rathe said.

"How can I tell which bailiff's men will exceed their authority?" Mirremay asked. "If Point of Hopes has a method, I'm not too proud to learn."

They could fence like this all day, Rathe thought, and her people would still be waiting when he and Eslingen left the station. Better to cut matters short. "There's a political dimension to this, you know."

Mirremay snorted. "Everything's political these days."

"Some things more than others," Rathe answered.

"Make your point, Rathe." Mirremay sounded almost amused, but Rathe was not deceived.

"The gold is untaxed," he said. "I'm sure van Duiren mentioned that there was coin involved, possibly even that it was gold, and maybe even that it hadn't paid the right dues, but have you thought about what that might mean, in the current situation?"

A faint frown appeared on Mirremay's face. "Go on," she said.

Rathe nodded to Eslingen. "He'll back me up on this. We've taken advice from the University on the matter, and untaxed gold can function like aurichalcum. It's weaker, but still dangerous, especially in large amounts. And after this summer—you can guess how the Surintendant is taking it."

"And who he might suspect," Mirremay said, with a glance at Eslingen. "Does he know who you're working with again?"

"It's an approved collaboration," Rathe said, and Eslingen smiled.

"And I believe you know, Chief Point, exactly how Master Caiazzo would use foreign gold," he said.

"I know at least one good reason that you yourself might need cash in hand," Rathe said. He waved to the room around them. "It can't have been cheap to bring this place up to standard."

"We're all very knowledgeable," Mirremay said. "And?"

"I know why Caiazzo wants the coin," Rathe began.

"And he's found the right coin to fee you properly," Mirremay said, and Rathe felt himself flush.

Eslingen said, lazily, "My principal feels the whole thing's too hot to handle, Chief Point. In consideration of which he's more than happy to cooperate with the points."

"One might have expected him to turn to me," Mirremay observed.

"I'm sure he trusts you," Eslingen said, in a tone that implied just the opposite.

Mirremay scowled, and Rathe said hastily, "Be that as it may, Chief Point, you and Caiazzo have one thing in common. Surintendant Fourie doesn't trust either one of you."

"That's hardly news," Mirremay said.

"He'd like an excuse," Rathe said. "And politics makes an excellent one. I respect the man enormously, but this time I think he's wrong. I can prove it's not Caiazzo if I have to, but you—I don't know about you, Chief. If you're backing van Duiren...."

"And would I tell you if I were?" Mirremay demanded.

"You'd tell me if you weren't," Rathe said.

"But would you believe me?" Mirremay shook her head. "Very well, Rathe, my cards on the table. First, my arrangements to fund the building here are solid and conventional and my own business. But it can be proved where the money came from, and that I haven't bankrupted myself in the process. Second, I'm no merchant-venturer, I've got no use for untaxed gold. On the other hand, the Queen pays treasure-trove on such coin, a full tenth of the value, and I'd have no objection to that fee or to improving my reputation. That's why I was willing to sign the bailiff's writ. But I don't hold with murder, and I can't afford politics, and I want nothing more to do with this mess." She gave a sudden, thin smile. "Unless you should call your point on my turf, Rathe, in which case I expect my full share of the fees and rewards."

"Of course," Rathe said. He thought he believed her, though he would probably ask one of the others at Point of Hopes to verify the finances—Pallanguey, maybe, she had friends among the clerks. "And I appreciate your candor, Chief Point."

"I'm glad we've reached an accord," Mirremay said. "And now—now I think we've wasted quite enough time on the matter." She straightened easily. "This way, Adjunct Point."

Rathe followed her down the station stairs and through the main room, Eslingen at his shoulder. The group that had confronted them in the street lounged by the double-stove, watchful as hounds. They were Mirremay's chosen team, Rathe recognized, her particular favorites, bound to her rather than to the station or any other loyalty. He gave them a careful look, wanting to be sure he'd know them again, and the woman—Chaudet, the junior Adjunct—gave him a feral grin.

"And I trust this will be the last we see of you, Adjunct Point," Mirremay said, her voice just loud enough to carry to every corner of the silent room. "Unless you come to share out the reward."

Rathe paused in the open door. "And to that end, I assume you'll encourage all cooperation."

Mirremay grinned. "A touch. Of course we would be happy to work with you—to that end."

"Thank you, Chief Point," Rathe said, and beat a hasty retreat.

They made their way back toward Point of Hopes through increasingly busy streets—ordinarily busy, Rathe was pleased to note, but he was also sure that they were being watched. They stopped again at Jascinte's Well, and Eslingen bought a cone of nuts from a young man with a roasting cart. Rathe looked over his shoulder, back the way they'd come, but saw no sign of of a tail. Probably the watchers had been set to see that they left Point of Knives, were even now heading back to Mirremay to report.

Eslingen held out the paper cone. "Next time you do something like that, you might warn me."

Rathe hesitated. "I didn't think it was going to go like that," he admitted. "If I'd thought—yeah, I would have warned you."

"She's dangerous, this Mirremay," Eslingen said. "And I thought the whole idea was to keep her from building her own little fiefdom in Point of Knives."

"Yes, she is," Rathe said. "And, yes, it was."

"It doesn't seem to have worked out all that well."

"Not the way the Surintendant planned, no." Rathe paused. "At least, probably not, anyway. He's a—complicated man."

"I don't like 'complicated,'" Eslingen said.

"Then you're in the wrong business," Rathe said.

For a moment, it hung in the balance, and then Eslingen's mouth twitched upward. "I'm a simple soldier, Adjunct Point—"

"You're about as simple as the epicycles of Arjent," Rathe said, and traced the looping corkscrew pattern in the air for emphasis.

Eslingen swept him a bow, graceful in spite of the cone still in one hand. "Why, that's the kindest thing you've ever said about me." He paused. "I meant it, you know."

"I know." Rathe said. "And next time, I will warn you. If I can."

Eslingen lifted an eyebrow. "That's the best you can do?"

"Yes." Rathe met his eyes squarely. "It's all I can promise, Philip."

There was a moment of stillness, the business of the square moving around them, as distant as if they stood encased in glass. Eslingen shrugged at last. "So. I'll take what I can get."

Rathe nodded, not knowing what to say. He only hoped that he hadn't spoiled everything.

Chapter Five
THE COUNTING HOUSE

ESLINGEN SETTLED HIMSELF by the tavern's fire and unfolded the broadsheets he'd picked up on his way through Temple Fair. By mutual if unspoken agreement, he and Rathe were both avoiding places where they were known individually, which left them mostly northriver places like this one. It was pleasant enough, occupied in the early evening primarily by clerks from the counting houses and factors' offices along the Mercandry. The prices were correspondingly higher, but it was worth it for the anonymity. No one here had cause to remember either Caiazzo's knife or the Adjunct Point at Point of Hopes.

He bespoke two plates of the night's ordinary, telling the waiter not to serve until his guest arrived, and turned his attention to the broadsheets. He'd bought a weekly almanac as well as a more personal sheet, and scanned it quickly, noting the positions of the major planets. The sun was in the Charioteer, and solidly aspected; the astrologer predicted quiet days and soft weather, plenty of time for the harvest and the last short-range trading ventures before winter closed the roads. His solar horoscope was equally benign, though he noted with a wry grin that the moon was in the Sea-bull, house of passion and illicit relationships. It would be nice if this affair lasted a bit longer than the moon's transit of the sign, but somehow he doubted it.

He folded the papers and tucked them into the cuff of his coat as he saw Rathe approach. The pointsman had shed his jerkin and truncheon, looked like any other southriver laborer in his rumpled coat and worn breeches. He looked a bit out of place, Eslingen thought, but no worse than the carter at the table in the corner: a man meeting friends of higher station, that was all.

"Any news?" he asked, as Rathe pulled out his chair.

"Some." Rathe reached for the wine that stood ready and poured himself a glass. "Biatris—the apprentice I had watching van Duiren's counting house—says it's in use, and that Delon is definitely the same person as van Duiren. She comes mostly in the late afternoon or evening, and rarely stays long. She's usually gone by sunset and always before second sunrise. Biatris hasn't seen her meeting with anyone, but she thinks van Duiren's been expecting someone the last day or so."

Eslingen frowned. He was starting to recognize Rathe's moods, would have expected him to be more pleased than this. "But?"

"Monteia's ordered Biatris off the job," Rathe said. "And I've been warned off as well. It seems the counting house is in Point of Knives."

Eslingen lifted an eyebrow. "I thought the crossroad—Lanyard Road?—was the boundary."

"It and Cockerel Row, yes. And so it is, in general practice," Rathe answered. "But the official writ runs one street further west, and Mirremay is claiming it."

"Damn."

"Yeah." Rathe gave a sour smile. "I'll give her the benefit of the doubt and say she's angling for the reward, but—it's inconvenient."

"Very." Eslingen topped up their glasses.

"I do have an idea," Rathe said, after a moment.

Eslingen gave him a wary look. He was beginning to suspect that not all of Rathe's ideas were as reasonable as they sounded on first hearing. "Oh?"

"Yeah," Rathe said again. "Biatris says the woman across the street rents rooms on her second floor. If we were quick and reasonably discreet, we could take one of those rooms, and the odds are fairly good that Mirremay's pets won't spot us."

Eslingen turned the idea over carefully in his mind, but couldn't see anything immediately wrong with it. "All right, that could work."

"We'll go tomorrow early," Rathe said. "My guess is van Duiren won't be active then, and Mirremay's people will slink home to report."

"Let's hope you're right," Eslingen said.

THEY MADE THEIR way through the side streets, avoiding Lanyard Road and the cross street until Rathe scouted ahead and reported no sign of Mirremay's people. The counting house was closed, its windows shuttered, but the house opposite was open, and a woman sat in the sun outside the main door, shelling peas into a bowl. Eslingen rested his hand on Rathe's shoulder.

"Let me. If any of Mirremay's people are still watching, I'm Caiazzo's man. She can take it up with him."

Rathe hesitated, then nodded. "Rent a front room. If it's clear, open the shutters. I'll join you then."

"Right." Eslingen handed him the basket he had been carrying—it held a jug of tea and a bottle of wine, bread and a pie for the long watch—and started briskly up the street.

The woman looked up at his approach, and Eslingen doffed his hat. "Good morning, dame."

"Morning—soldier?"

Eslingen bowed. "Just so. And on leave, and wondering if you still rented rooms. A friend of mine said you might."

"I do," she said.

"It was a particular room I wanted," Eslingen said. "One that overlooks the street."

She gave him a measuring look—summing up, Eslingen thought, just how much damage he and his lover were likely to do to the room, whether points would be called, and whether his money was good, and then shrugged one shoulder.

"There's a front room available. But the furniture's extra."

"I don't need much," Eslingen answered, with perfect truth. "And I don't know how long I'll stay."

She nodded. Her hands never slowed, stripping the peas from their pods. "A seilling a day, and another for a bed and mattress."

"Not per day," Eslingen said.

She shook her head grudgingly. "For a week, if you stay so long."

"Throw in a couple of stools, and it's done." Eslingen gave her his most winning smile.

She lifted an eyebrow, but nodded. "Agreed. Payment in advance, soldier."

Eslingen fished in his purse, came up with the coins. "I'll be back within the hour, dame."

They spent the time at a teahouse, sadly not in the well-tended garden, but in the smoky main room, where Rathe could, with effort, peer out the shutters and catch a glimpse of van Duiren's counting house. Eslingen lifted an eyebrow, and Rathe shrugged.

"I can't afford to get in bad with Monteia just at the moment. And Monteia can't afford to annoy Mirremay."

"Awkward," Eslingen agreed.

"And if I were Mirremay, I'd want my people back watching by now."

"They've been there all night," Eslingen said, in what he hoped were soothing tones. "Surely they need some sleep."

"Damn it." Rathe let the shutter close. "Apparently not. I just saw Chaudet wandering up the street."

"Damn," Eslingen said. "All right. I'll take the room and you can come in the back door."

"You're not exactly unrecognizable," Rathe said.

"It's a different coat," Eslingen said. He'd decided he didn't want to risk his best clothes on this particular assignment. "And I'll let my hair down." He suited the action to the words, taking off his hat and loosening his hair from its tie.

Rathe lifted his eyebrows. "You look—dissipated."

"Why, thank you, Adjunct Point." Eslingen grinned. "Perhaps we could arrange to make it less of a pretense?"

"We've a watch to keep," Rathe answered, not without regret, and the nearest tower clock struck the quarter hour.

"The room should be ready," Eslingen said, and picked up the basket, tucking it under one arm. A different coat, hair loose and untidy, a common-looking basket in his hands…. "Well?" he asked, and Rathe nodded.

"You'll do. Open the shutter when you're settled and I'll come in by the garden door."

Eslingen saw no sign of Mirremay's people as he made his way up the street, felt none of the prickle at the back of the neck that meant someone was paying too close attention. The landlady was within, but her maidservant handed him the key and promised to let his lover in the kitchen door so that his mistress wouldn't know how he was spending his day off. The room itself was much as he'd expected, the sort of room he'd commandeered a hundred times on campaign, bare and faintly dusty, with a heavy bedstead in one corner piled with what proved at the touch to be a straw mattress. Fairly fresh straw, at least, he thought, and pulled back the shutter for the signal.

He left the basket in a shaded corner, and dragged one stool to the side of the window, so that he could see the street and the counting house without being seen. A few minutes later, Rathe arrived, slipping the maidservant a coin and bolting the door behind him.

"What in Astree's name did you tell them?"

"That you were houseman to an elderly merchant resident who was enamored of your manly charms," Eslingen answered promptly. "And desperately jealous. But I saw you from afar, and managed to seduce you away for these few days of my leave, but we don't dare be seen for fear you'd lose your place."

"Idiot." Rathe shook his head. "That wasn't even a good play."

"I got it out of a broadsheet," Eslingen answered. He shifted so that he could lean against the wall and still keep an eye on the street. "What now?"

"This is the boring part," Rathe answered, and dragged the other stool to the opposite side of the window. "We wait."

"Ah." Eslingen scanned the street, empty except for a lop-eared dog nosing at a puddle beside the wall opposite. Even as he watched, the dog lifted its head and trotted off. Eslingen sighed. "For how long?"

Rathe grinned. "Until something happens. Or until we're sure nothing's going to happen."

"Lovely." Eslingen rested his head against the wall. "We could play cards—"

Rathe shook his head. "I don't carry a deck."

"Dice?"

Rathe shook his head again. "Besides, we don't want to be distracted."

"Which rules out my next suggestion," Eslingen said, with a grin.

"If you can keep watch under those circumstances, I'll be offended," Rathe answered.

"All right, probably not," Eslingen conceded. "Still, it would make the time pass."

"No," Rathe said.

"Are you sure?"

"Positive." Rathe paused. "How in Tyrseis's name did you end up a soldier?"

"I ran off to be a horseboy in a mercenary regiment when I was thirteen," Eslingen answered promptly. "It was better than being a horseboy in an inn for the rest of my life. At least there was a chance of promotion. How'd you end up a pointsman?"

Rathe shrugged. "We lived near the station at Point of Hearts when I was a boy. I began as a runner, just looking to make a few demmings, and discovered I was good at the work. And I liked it. One of the local advocates paid my 'prentice-fee, and—that was that."

It was on the tip of Eslingen's tongue to say something about Rathe's stars, but he swallowed the words. Rathe was right not to tell him, and it was his right to keep the secret, and that was the end of it. "And evidently the chance of promotion is just as good as in the regiment," he said instead, and Rathe shrugged.

"Good enough. Though I got this post early, I'm likely to stay an adjunct point for quite a while."

They lapsed into silence. Eslingen watched the shadows turn and lengthen, stretching across the dusty street. Mirremay's people paid the neighborhood another visit, pacing the length of the street, but didn't stay, and by the time the clock struck four, they'd disappeared again. After a while, Rathe shared out some of the bread and tea. Eslingen took his share, more to have something to do than because he was hungry, and then, as the sun settled behind the chimney pots, he cut them both wedges from the pie. It was excellent, and Eslingen was debating a second slice when he saw Rathe straighten.

"Van Duiren."

Eslingen checked the impulse to lean forward to look, waited instead until she came into his field of view. Sure enough, it was the woman who had claimed to be Old Steen's wife, though she was dressed now in a plain skirt and bodice, a long sleeveless coat open over the rest of the outfit.

"Pawnbroker's coat," Rathe said, and Eslingen glanced at him.

Rathe grinned. "It's got hidden pockets and a few spells woven in, or most of them do. The dishonest ones will palm your goods and give you back a reasonable facsimile that will last just long enough for them to get away."

"The things I learn from you…." Eslingen shook his head..

On the street below, van Duiren fumbled with her keys, first the main lock, and then a smaller, inner lock. She pushed back the door and disappeared into the shop, and a few moments later the shutters began to open.

"Isn't it a bit late in the day to open a counting house?" Eslingen asked. "I'd think keeping the doors open after sunset would be an invitation to trouble, with second sunrise not coming for another hour—especially if she keeps cash on hand."

"It would be, normally," Rathe said. "But if she's a fence, she's got connections that will protect her—not least of which would be Mirremay—or this is just the place where she has the preliminary meetings. Or she's up to something else entirely. But, no, I don't really expect to find your gold in there."

"Pity, that," Eslingen said, and stopped abruptly. "Look there."

"I see him." Rathe fumbled in his purse, came up with a small telescope, the kind artillerymen used to train their guns. He focussed on the stranger, a man in a scholar's long robe, and shook his head as the man ducked into van Duiren's shop. "Well, that's something to tell Maseigne Vair. A Demean by his hood, too, though I didn't get a decent look at his badge."

"The badges are—?" Eslginen cocked his head.

"What branch or house he's affiliated with within the University," Rathe answered.

"Seems a bit unsubtle to go walking around like that," Eslingen said.

"Yeah, the thought had crossed my mind," Rathe said. "It could be a decoy—wait, hello."

This time Eslingen did risk leaning forward just a little. A woman was coming down the street, a well-dressed woman in a neat brimless cap, a closed parasol balanced on her shoulder. Rathe had his glass out, peering through it as she paused at the counting house door, and Eslingen heard the sigh of satisfaction.

"Faculty of Sciences and Herathean House. Even if I hadn't gotten a good look at her face, that will help identify her."

Eslingen looked back at the counting house. Lamps glowed in its windows as the dusk closed in, the hour of full dark between the setting of the true sun and the rising of the winter-sun. Occasionally a shadow moved across the light, but it was impossible to see any details. All too soon, it seemed, the front door opened again, and the two scholars left together, the woman using her parasol now as a walking stick.

"Do we follow?" he asked, and Rathe shook his head.

"Too late, damn it. I should have thought."

A moment later, the last of the lamps went out, and Rathe swore under his breath. Van Duiren emerged a moment later, carefully locked the doors behind her, and started away in the opposite direction. Rathe shook his head.

"Well, at least we know she's using the place for meetings—and that there's a University connection. Maseigne Vair will be glad to know."

Eslingen took a deep breath. "Maybe Young Steen had the right of it."

Rathe looked at him. "What do you mean?"

"Well, not quite the way he'd do it," Eslingen amended. "But he thought we should break in and search the place—him and me, he meant, not you and I."

"That's illegal, you know, Lieutenant." Rathe shook his head. "And I can't think of a better idea."

THE FRONT OF the counting house was hopelessly exposed, but there was bound to be a back door, if only for the night-soil man. Rathe found the alley without difficulty, and stepped into its deeper shadows. In the darkness, Eslingen's shirtcuffs seemed unnaturally bright, and Rathe was glad of his own oversized coat. It wasn't fashionable, but it did help to hide his presence. He touched Eslingen's shoulder.

"It's the fourth house on the left," he said softly, and saw the other man nod.

They picked their way along the rutted street, through mud that smelled of rotting cabbage, and Rathe glanced over his shoulder at the houses behind them. Fortunately, the alley was only used for garbage, and the smell meant that most of them kept their doors and windows shut tight, and Rathe turned his attention to the counting house door. It bore a massive lock with a tiny keyhole, the kind of magistically warded lock that its maker's guild proclaimed "unbreakable" and he made a sour face. The only good thing was that it probably meant the door wasn't barred as well.

"And how do you propose to get past that?" Eslingen asked. He looked up at the windows on the upper floor. "I could probably climb in there, but it wouldn't exactly be subtle."

Rathe reached into his purse again, came up with the ring of keys he'd had made from the wax impressions he'd taken from Old Steen's belongings. He held them up in the dim light, studying the wards, chose three that looked as though they might fit. It was likely he'd have to resort to picks, or his universal key, but he thought there was a chance Old Steen might have been twisty enough to have keys to this back door. He tested them quickly: all the right size, one even magistically active, but none were meant for the particular lock. He put them away, and pulled out his universal key. Well, not exactly his; he'd taken it off a serial burglar who'd plagued Point of Hopes some four years past, part of the man's elaborate and magistically active toolkit. All of it had been slated to be melted down to keep it from falling into improper hands, but that had seemed a waste of something so cleverly made as the universal key, and Rathe had discreetly pocketed it. Three or four more items had gone missing, all equally useful and Monteia had said nothing when they didn't reach the fire.

"This should do it," he said, and turned the bezel at the top, setting the solar and lunar positions in the tiny orrery. The key chimed once, the sound almost inaudible, and he adjusted the size of the wards to fit the opening.

"That's never standard issue," Eslingen said.

Rathe snorted. "Not hardly." He slipped the key into the lock, probing for the tumblers. He could feel the warded lock resisting, the key sliding from the spelled surface, but then the key's magic caught and coiled in the gaps of the ward, easing it away, and the key slipped securely into the tumblers. Rathe turned it carefully, gave a sigh of satisfaction as the lock gave way. He pushed gently, hoping there was no bar, and the door swung open before him.

"You continue to amaze me," Eslingen said, and together they slipped inside.

Rathe closed the door softly behind them, and they stood for a moment in the dark, listening for any sign that they were not alone. There was nothing, no sound, no breath of air, not even the smell of cooking, just the faint bitter scent of a stove long unused and uncleaned. Eslingen moved first, his eyes adjusting to the light, and Rathe heard the gentle clicks as he tested the shutters.

"Strike a light if they're solid," Rathe said, and a moment later light bloomed as Eslingen lit a candle end. Van Duiren's, Rathe noted, taken from a box on the windowsill, and that meant they'd better be quick, or she might notice a missing candle.

"Not much of a housekeeper," Eslingen said.

Rathe glanced around the bare room. Even in the candle's uncertain light, it was possible to tell that the floor hadn't been swept in weeks, and the stove was chipped, its door sagging open. "Well, we know she doesn't live here."

"Or make much pretense of it, either," Eslingen said. He held the candle high so as not to dazzle them.

"I supposed there's not much need," Rathe said. But there ought to be, she ought to be doing everything possible to keep van Duiren and Delon separate, and if that meant the expense of extra servants and wood for the fire, it should be worth it. Unless she'd never intended it to be more than a superficial disguise, and that didn't make sense, either. There was something wrong here, he could almost taste it, something that he was missing, and something wrong in the house, too…. He held his breath for a moment, feeling the air on his face, listening for any sound, even the softest of movements from within. But there was nothing at all, nothing to justify the sense of unease, and he worked his shoulders, annoyed with his own unease.

"The front room," he said.

Eslingen cupped his hand around the candle, shielding the light, and Rathe nodded. "I'll go first."

The shutters at the front of the house were closed and locked as well, but Rathe found a firescreen beside the stove and set it to shield the single lamp before he allowed Eslingen to light it. This larger room, at least, looked more normal, the stove old but recently cleaned, a clerk's slanted table braced against one wall. There was a smaller table as well, flanked by a set of cushioned stools. A teapot stood upside down on the shelf above it.

"No ledgers," Eslingen said, and Rathe shot him a glance. The Leaguer was developing an eye for the essentials—or, more likely, he'd looted enough businesses to know what to look for.

"And nothing on the clerk's table." Rathe checked the inkwell—only a quarter full—and the quill lying beside it was badly trimmed. The cake of red ink was dry and cracked: a better pretense than in the empty kitchen, but still not one that was meant to deceive a careful eye. There was no book-presss, no clock, not even a chest, only an unlocked paper-box on shelf above the clerk's table. He opened it anyway, and found it half full of inexpensive paper; when he rifled through it, he saw without surprise that every sheet was blank.

"What now?" Eslingen asked.

"Upstairs," Rathe said. That was where the strongroom should be, if in fact there was one. He picked up the lamp, leaving Eslingen to collect the candle, and started up the narrow stairs.

There were two rooms on the upper floors, and it was instantly obvious which was the strongroom. That door was bound in iron and it was fitted with another warded lock. Rathe pushed open the other one anyway, to reveal a chamber empty except for a traveler's chest. He heard Eslingen's breath catch, and shook his head.

"No lock."

"Damn."

"Check it anyway," Rathe said, and turned his attention to the strong-room door.

The wards on this lock were stronger, tuned not to the usual solar indices, but to the cycles of Heira, and it took him a few minutes to adjust the key's orrery to catch the spell. He made the last change, and felt the wards give, the key finally meshing with the tumblers. He felt for the lock, eased it open, and looked over to see Eslingen on his feet again beside the open trunk.

"Any luck?"

"Nothing. Old clothes and an out-of-season hat."

Even though he hadn't expected anything better, Rathe felt a twinge of disappointment. Just once, it would have been nice to have the solution just tumble into his lap. He killed the thought and pushed open the strongroom door. The single window was heavily shuttered, and when Eslingen tapped it, it had the heavy ring of iron. Rathe lit the two standing lamps and scanned the narrow space as the light swelled. It was typical enough, shelves on both the side walls, and a table in the center of the room, far enough back from the window that no one could see in, but still close enough to catch the best of the light. There was a brassbound cashbox beneath the window—fitted with yet another warded lock, Rathe noted—and there were at least a dozen ledgers on the walls. He suppressed a groan at the sight. They were a solid night's work on their own, and he wasn't prepared— And if he found the gold's location, what then? He couldn't give it to Caiazzo, and he didn't want to claim it for Mirremay. Give it to Monteia, he supposed, though the resulting fight would be fierce.

And that was another profitless thought. He looked at Eslingen. "You start on the books—the newest first, I think. I'll open the cash box."

"Is there anything in particular I'm looking for?" Eslingen asked, and took down the nearest leder.

"I wish I knew," Rathe said frankly. He knelt beside the cashbox, looking from the lock to his key and back again. "Anything out of the ordinary."

"Which I'll only be able to tell you after I've read the lot," Eslignen muttered.

"Why do you think I gave you the job?" Rathe frowned thoughtfully at the cash box. There was a monogram scratched on the lid above the lock, an "S" rather than anything that could match van Duiren's aliases, and he took out the ring of Old Steen's keys again. Sure enough, the largest of the keys matched the lock. "Old Steen had a key to fit—no, this was his box, but why she's left it here—"

"A lure?" Eslingen asked.

"Possibly. Though what she'd gain from it...." Rathe shook his head, and lifted the lid, not surprised to see a mix of coin, more silver than gold. They were jumbled together, not separated out like most merchants' hoards, and he ran a hand through the mess, dredging up enough gold coins to sort out a few foreign pieces. They all bore a customs mark, however, and he sat back on his heels, sighing.

"No luck?" Eslingen said.

"No." Rathe shook his head. "You?"

"No." Eslingen paused. "Well, she could be hiding any number of frauds in her ledgers, I'm no clerk. But I haven't seen anything that looks like a sudden influx of money, and I certainly haven't found anything that might be notes from Old Steen about where he hid his treasure."

"Damn it," Rathe said. It was all wrong, the whole thing. There should be more here, or considerably less, and yet if it was some kind of lure, what was it meant to bring? Them? He tipped his head to the side, considering the idea. He couldn't quite see what van Duiren would gain by it—she already knew he was working against her, he'd made that clear when she first brought her claim to Point of Hopes. And she must know by now that Caiazzo had fee'd Monteia to place his knife with the points, so what she could hope to gain…. But it was too late for that to matter. They'd taken her bait, and now the main thing was to extricate themselves as discreetly and painlessly as possible.

"This doesn't feel right," Eslingen said, and set the last ledger back in its place. "It just doesn't make sense."

"No more it does," Rathe answered. "I don't know why, but I think she wanted us to break in—maybe just to find nothing."

"If she wants us here," Eslingen began, and Rathe nodded.

"I think we'd be wiser to be somewhere else." He closed the chest again, letting the lock close, the wards reforming with a heavy snap. "We'll put back everything we can as we go, but the main thing is to leave. Now."

THEY SWEPT BACK down the stairs and though the house, Rathe in the lead with the lamp, Eslingen behind him with the candle end. In the front room, Rathe restored the firescreen to its place and set the lamp back on its shelf, cupping his hand to blow out the light. That left them with only the single candle to survey the empty kitchen, and then Eslingen licked his fingers and pinched out the flame, stood holding it as the wax solidified.

"If she looks closely—if she has reason to look—she'll know someone's been here," he said.

"Yeah," Rathe said, unhappily. "And she'll be able to see that I've manipulated her locks. But it's too late to worry about that now."

The candle had cooled enough, and Eslingen set it back in its box. "And what about those people from the University?"

Rathe eased back the door, peered out into the alley. "That's a good question. Were they even from the University, or were they just more bait?"

I hadn't thought of that. Eslingen swallowed the words, and slipped past Rathe into the alley, scanning the street to either side. There was no sign of another presence, no movement in the shadows; when he looked up, the windows were all shuttered and nothing moved on the rooftops. Behind him there was a soft, heavy click as the lock resealed itself, and

Rathe straightened, pocketing his key. Eslingen turned, ready to retrace his steps, but Rathe caught his sleeve, and pointed in the other direction. Eslingen nodded, and fell in at the pointsman's shoulder, following him down the narrow street.

The winter-sun had risen, and Lanyard Road was bright enough to see shadows. Eslingen heard the sound of hooves and the low rumble of wheels at the crossroads, saw a cart pull slowly past, the driver hunched on the seat. Otherwise, the street was empty: this was not a neighborhood where people gathered after dark. Rathe turned right, heading south; this was not the most direct route to Point of Hopes, and Eslingen glanced curiously at the other man.

"I'd just as soon not go straight home," Rathe said. "And there will still be traffic on Customs Road."

"You think we're being followed?" Eslingen just managed to keep himself from looking over his shoulder.

"I don't know," Rathe said.

They walked in silence for a while longer, Eslingen straining to hear footsteps behind them. There was nothing, just once the distant sound of another cart, and another time the cackle of fowl disturbed at roost, but he couldn't shake the nagging feeling that someone was there. And that was asking for trouble, asking for tight-strung nerves to make a man go off half-cocked, and he rolled his shoulders as though that would shed the sense that they were being watched.

"Do you think they weren't from the University, those people?" he asked.

Rathe shrugged. "I don't know," he said again. "And, thank Dis, it's not my problem. I'll send word to Vair and let her deal with it."

"Nice that something isn't," Eslingen said, and that drew a fugitive grin.

"I have enough on my book right now, yes, thank you."

Customs Road was busier, lanterns lit in front of the taverns and the few late-working chandlers; a string of mage-fire globes framed the bathhouse at the Sandureigne. Eslingen gave it a wistful glance—a hot bath and cold beer sounded deeply appealing—but matched Rathe's easy pace. In the crowd, it was easier to find an excuse to look back and sideways, but he saw no real sign that they were being followed, only the usual mix of night-working women and those bound for home and bed. A string of four horses plodded up the middle of the street, pack frames piled high, a wicker cradle strapped onto the lead horse's frame. Bells jingled softly, counterpoint to the sound of the hooves, and the baby slept, oblivious. A late arrival or an early departure, it was impossible to tell which, and they disappeared around a curve of the road.

Past the Sandureigne, the crowds thinned again, the road passing between shuttered shops and houses that showed lights only on their uppermost floors. Rathe glanced over his shoulder again, and took the first right hand turning. Eslingen cocked his head to listen, but heard nothing, not even the wheels of a cart or a porter's bells.

"I've got a feeling," Rathe said softly, sounding almost embarrassed. "We're being watched."

"I haven't spotted anyone," Eslingen said.

"No more have I," Rathe admitted. "But—"

"If you say so, that's word enough for me," Eslingen said. He could feel the itching between his shoulder blades now, too, the unnatural certainty that he was under observation. "Do we split up, draw them out? Or I could fall back, see if I could spot them."

"I don't want to split up," Rathe said. "For one thing, I've no idea how many of them there might be."

"Then we find a spot," Eslingen said. "You know the city better than I do, you call it, but—a place where we can drop into shadow, out of their sight, and see if they come up."

"And then what?"

Kill them. Eslingen swallowed his first suggestion, said, more moderately, "Get a good look at them, for a start. Grab them and beat some answers out of them if we can."

Rathe nodded slowly. "What my old chief point would say to the idea, I don't know."

"From what I've seen of your current chief, she'd be hefting a big stick herself," Eslingen said.

Rathe grinned. "True enough. Monteia's very—direct in her ways." He sobered quickly. "Once we cross Bakers' Row, the road splits. We'll take the right fork, and almost immediately there's an alley to the right. We'll duck in there and see what happens."

Eslingen nodded. He could almost hear movement behind them now as the city quieted, the occasional faint scrape of a shoe on cobbles, a click that might have been a cudgel carried unwarily, or might only have been imagination. He knew better than to look back, but he could see the tension in Rathe's shoulders, the pointsman's movements every bit as tight as his own.

Ahead, the road forked, and it took all his willpower not to pick up the pace, but he kept walking, his head bent a little as though he were listening to some fascinating story. They took the right fork, Rathe leading them casually to the right-hand side of the street, and, sure enough, the road curved still further, cutting off the view of anyone following them.

"Now," Rathe said quietly, and they slipped together into the mouth of the alley. Eslingen pressed his back against the wall, flattening himself into the darkest part of the shadows; Rathe leaned beside him, his head turned to watch the street beyond. They stood there for a hundred heartbeats, another hundred, and still another. Rathe shifted slightly, trying to see beyond the end of the building, but there was no movement. Then at last there was the sound of hooves and the rumble of wheels, and another cart rolled into view. By the sound of it, it was empty, but Rathe took a step forward to get a better look. The movement drew the carter's eye, and he gave a yelp, seeing them lurking in the alley. He flourished his whip, urging the horse to a heavy trot, and in spite of himself Eslingen snickered.

"You should be ashamed of yourself, Adjunct Point, frightening a law-abiding man like that."

"What makes you think he's law-abiding?" Rathe said, and shook his head. "I'd say that wasn't our man."

"It doesn't seem likely," Eslingen agreed. "What now?"

"They must have gotten suspicious," Rathe said, "guessed what we were going to try. Damn it, I'd have liked to get a look at them."

"We could backtrack a bit," Eslingen said, doubtfully.

"They're long gone," Rathe said. "No, we might as well go home. There's nothing more for us here."

"But not by the most direct route," Eslingen suggested, and Rathe grinned.

"And I thought I had the nasty suspicious mind."

"We're two of a kind," Eslingen said.

They spend another three-quarters of an hour making their way back to Rathe's lodgings, but Eslingen was sure within minutes that whoever had been following them was gone. It took Rathe longer to be certain, or at least longer to admit it, but finally they slipped into the courtyard below Rathe's stair. Eslingen stood listening a final time while Rathe re-locked the gate, and shrugged as Rathe gave him a questioning glance.

"Nothing. I haven't felt as though we were being followed, either, not since we tried to draw them out."

"Me neither." Rathe shook his head. "Come on, let's fetch water and go to bed."

"Water?"

"For bathing," Rathe said. He was, Eslingen thought, unexpectedly fastidious for someone who generally looked as though he'd slept in his clothes.

"The bathhouse at the Sandureigne has marble floors," Eslingen said. "A hot pool and a cold, and masseurs with hands like tree-roots...."

"What you've got is a washbasin," Rathe said briskly, and heaved on the well-rope. Eslingen caught the bucket, emptied it into the pail that stood waiting.

"What about the massage?"

Rathe glanced over his shoulder. "You'll have to earn that."

"At your service," Eslingen murmured, and followed up him the stairs.

Chapter Six
BEST-LAID PLANS

RATHE WOKE A little after the day-sun's rise, built up the fire and had just set water to boil when he heard the voices from the courtyard. He glanced quickly out the window, saw Jiemen and Mirremay's adjunct Chaudet just closing the gate, and swore under his breath.

"Philip!" He crossed quickly to the bed, but Eslingen was already sitting up, awake and alert in an instant.

"What?"

Rathe scooped up the other man's clothes, thrust them into his arms. "Chaudet. Through there—" He pointed to the alcove that served as his storeroom, and Eslingen obeyed, not stopping to dress. "She's got Jiemen with her, and whatever's going on—I don't have a good feeling about this."

"Right." Eslingen pulled his shirt over his head. "Is there a back way out?"

"No." Rathe caught the lifted eyebrow, and shrugged. "I didn't want a place with a back way in."

"You may want to rethink that," Eslingen said, and backed into the narrow space. Rathe pulled the painted screen across it, and braced himself for the knock at the door.

"Adjunct Point?" Jiemen's tone was scrupulously polite. "Sorry to bother you, but it's urgent."

Rathe gave the room a last glance, saw nothing that would betray Eslingen's presence, and unfastened the latch. "What is it?"

"Is Philip Eslingen here?" Chaudet asked.

Rathe shook his head, unblushing. "What's wrong?"

"Dame van Duiren's sworn a charge against him," Jiemen said.

"On what grounds?" Rathe asked. He reached for his coat, shrugging it onto his shoulders. The sooner they were out of his rooms, the less chance there was that Eslingen would betray himself.

"She says he tried to kill her last night," Chaudet said. "Presumably at Master Caiazzo's behest, but that's not a point she can claim, at least not yet."

"But—" Rathe closed his lips firmly over his automatic protest. With Mirremay involved, it was better not to show his hand immediately. Not to mention that an alibi that consisted of 'I know Eslingen wasn't trying to kill anyone because I was with him and we were robbing a counting house that just happens to belong to Dame van Duiren under another name' wasn't likely to impress anyone. "Is it just her word? She's got a court case against Caiazzo, you know. And he has a countersuit, last I heard. That's not what I'd call reliable witness." He was moving toward the door as he spoke, collecting his truncheon and leather jerkin as he went.

"Her word and her knife's," Chaudet said. "They saw him clearly, and he's not an unnoticeable man."

"Still," Rathe said.

Chaudet shrugged. Jiemen said, "The chief was hoping you might speak for him."

"I can for some of the night," Rathe said, with caution. 'I was in bed with the man' wasn't much better as far as alibis went, and even less likely to be believed than burglary.

"In any case," Chaudet said, "Mirremay wants a word."

Rathe slanted a glance at Jiemen, who shrugged.

"I'm to go along with you," she said. "The chief's orders."

"Right," Rathe said. He moved closer to the door, herding the others out onto the landing, paused to lock the door behind him. Eslingen would have to fend for himself.

It was a bright day, clear, with a few high clouds and a northwesterly wind sweeping down from the river, bringing the first touch of the winter to come. Chaudet shivered and turned up her collar, the first sign of weakness Rathe had seen in her, and Jiemen fished in her pocket for a pair of half-gloves. Rathe jammed his hands into his pockets, hunching his shoulders to the wind, and looked again at Jiemen.

"The chief's sure about this?"

"Van Duiren came to us with a knife slice along her ribs and a swollen jaw where someone knocked her down," Chaudet said. "It's hard to argue with that."

Rathe nodded reluctantly. It wasn't impossible, he'd known accusers to mark themselves before now, but it argued a certain desperation. "Has her case been heard?"

Chaudet shot him a glance. "Funny you should ask that, Rathe. Caiazzo's managed to get the whole lot impounded, locked up in the back of the advocate's chambers."

Rathe shrugged. "Seems significant, that's all."

The main room at Point of Knives was unexpectedly crowded, Mirremay's second adjunct standing on a stool to shout down half a dozen women and men who faced off across the width of the room. They seemed to be arguing about short measure, and Chaudet gave them a wide berth.

"Upstairs," she said.

Mirremay's workroom was an oasis of quiet after the noise downstairs. The stove was lit, a kettle simmering on the hob while one of the station's apprentices tended the teapot, and a thin stick of incense helped drive back the smells of the street. Van Duiren reclined on the daybed, a damp cloth against her jaw, while a serious-looking young physician took her pulse. The bruise was real enough, Rathe saw instantly; her bodice was cut, and there was blood on the fabric, but it looked as though her stays had turned the worst of the blade. Mirremay had been leaning against the end of her worktable, while her secretary took dictation, but she pushed herself upright as they entered.

"Rathe. Chaudet told you our news?"

"Yes." Rathe glanced again at van Duiren. "I hope you're not badly hurt, dame?"

"No thanks to your friend," the merchant retorted. "It's just lucky I wasn't killed."

"Where is Lieutenant Eslingen?" Mirremay asked.

"I've no idea," Rathe answered.

"He wasn't there," Chaudet said, and Jiemen nodded.

"I'll vouch for that, chief."

Mirremay lifted an eyebrow. "You astonish me."

"And in the meantime, I'm set upon in the streets," van Duiren interjected. "And I have paid my fees, Chief Point."

"Indeed you have," Mirremay said, "and we'll get to the bottom of this. Rathe. What do you know of Eslingen's movements yesterday?"

"Most of the day we were together," Rathe said, cautiously. "We dined together, too."

"And after?" van Duiren demanded. She sat up, holding the sliced pieces of her bodice together. "What of the night?"

Mirremay didn't bother to suppress her grin, but she said, "Dame, you should be abed. Isn't that right, Doctor?"

The physician dipped his head. He bore a Demean badge at the collar of his plain blue robe—but then, Rathe thought, a Demean doctor was more likely to cooperate with Mirremay than was a Phoeban. "Indeed she should, Chief Point. And if you'll permit me, Dame, I'll see you home and safely settled."

There was no arguing with that, though for a moment Rathe thought van Duiren would try. But then she sighed, and let the doctor help her to her feet. "Perhaps you're right. But I stand by my charge, Chief Point."

"We'll find him," Mirremay promised, and the doctor helped her away. The noise from the main room was suddenly louder, the argument continuing, and after a moment Chaudet moved to close the door. Mirremay leaned back against the edge of her table.

"You really don't know where he is, Rathe?"

"I do not," Rathe answered promptly. "However, while I hesitate to call a woman of Dame van Duiren's stature a liar—"

"Oh, go right ahead," Mirremay said. "My guess is she cut herself, and paid one of her carters to take a swing at her."

Rathe paused. "Then—forgive me, chief, but why accept the charge?"

Mirremay looked down her nose at him, and Rathe lifted his hands. She was after the gold herself, she'd never made any bones about it even if she did plan to turn it in for the reward, and this was her way of letting van Duiren lead her to it.

"Sorry, I'm slow this morning."

"You should get more sleep," Mirremay said.

"So you can speak to Eslingen's whereabouts?" Chaudet asked.

"Yes, the night long," Rathe answered. "But, Chief Point, if you want to find what van Duiren's hiding, I have a proposal for you. Call the point, arrest Eslingen—and give her the rope to hang herself."

Mirremay nodded slowly, but Chaudet gave him a distinctly disapproving look.

"I wouldn't care to share your bed, Rathe."

"Philip's no fool," Rathe said. "He'll understand." He only hoped it was true.

ESLINGEN WAITED UNTIL he heard the lock catch and the footsteps retreat from the door before he shrugged himself into the rest of his clothes. He very much didn't like the sound of those charges—attacking a respectable merchant was the sort of thing that Astreianters took very seriously, most of them being merchants, respectable and not—and he liked even less being left to fend for himself while Rathe went off to deal with Mirremay. It reminded him unpleasantly of how he'd ended up working for Caiazzo in the first place: he'd been forced to shoot a man to protect the tavern where he'd been working, and even though it was self-defense, he'd spend a night in the cells at Point of Sighs. When he'd been released, the tavern keeper had declined to take him back, and Rathe had taken the opportunity to place him into Caiazzo's household just in case Caiazzo had been behind the missing children. He hadn't been, or at least his involvement had been unintentional, but—Rathe seemed to have a knack for creating awkward situations, at least for other people.

He fastened his stock, not bothering with a fancy knot, and slipped from the alcove still in his shirtsleeves. The points were long gone, the garden empty, and he took the time to cut himself a couple of slices of bread and cheese. He couldn't stay here, not if Rathe wasn't going to give him an alibi—though, to be fair, neither of the options were likely to inspire a great deal of confidence—but there was also no point in leaving until he had a destination in mind. There had been woodcuts of him and Rathe after the midsummer rescue of the children; people still recognized him now and then, and the points would certainly have a decent description.

That meant he should probably warn Caiazzo that this exercise in cooperating with the points was not going entirely as anticipated. He stuffed the last of the bread into his mouth, and stooped to peer at himself in the mirror. He hadn't shaved yet, and he wouldn't; unshaven and with his hair loose, his clothes fastened carelessly, he might pass without notice. And he could cross to the north side of the river, make his way to Customs Point along the opposite bank. It would add an hour or two to the journey, but he wouldn't have to cross the districts where he was best known.

He adjusted his hat to shadow his eyes, and let himself out of Rathe's rooms. The courtyard was empty of people, though he could hear the clack of the weaver's loom from the room by the gate, and her goat was grazing lazily on its tie. He shut the gate gently behind him, and started for the Hopes-Point Bridge.

The streets were growing busy, he saw with relief, women heading out on the business of the day, merchants to their shops and counting houses, servants bound for the early markets, even a sprinkling of gray-robed students heading home from a night in Point of Dreams. Eslingen let himself fall in behind one such group, still sleepily giggling to each other, and hoped to blend in with the crowd.

The pace slowed as they approached the foot of the bridge. That was unusual: Hopes-Point was broad enough to allow two carriages to pass side-by-side and still leave room for pedestrians, and Eslingen slowed his pace, pausing to consider the gem-like fruits laid out in a greengrocer's tray. He slanted a glance up the street, and saw the cause of the delay. A pair of pointsmen stood at the entrance to the bridge, just where the road sloped up to meet the first of the shops that perched on the bridge itself. Eslingen swallowed a curse—of course Rathe's people were good, and if Rathe was helping them—but surely he wouldn't be. He smiled and shook his head at the watchful grocer, and turned back to the south.

The movement drew attention, as he'd feared it might, running counter to the majority of the crowd. He hunched his shoulders, trying to look shorter and older, but he could feel the eyes on him, scowls turning to curiosity as he kept pushing south.

"Hey!"

Eslingen glanced over his shoulder, saw one of the pointsmen stepping away from his place. He tried to look away again, as though it had been only casual curiosity, as though the shout meant nothing to him, but even as he turned his head, he saw the other pointsman lift his truncheon.

"Stop that man."

Eslingen curbed himself sharply, looked around as though he had no idea to whom they referred. For a moment, he thought he'd bought enough time to get around the nearest corner, but then the second points-man shouted again.

"That man, the one in the blue hat! Stop him!"

This time, people did turn, did stare, surprise turning to suspicion. Eslingen cursed once, and bolted, forcing his way through the crowd. Some-one grabbed at his coat-tails, but he pulled free, ducking under the nose of a startled cart horse, darted down the far side of the street. A whistle shrilled behind him, and the raucous sound of a watchman's rattle rose above the sudden hubbub, calling reinforcements.

Eslingen swore again, ducked blindly down the first side street, and reversed his course at the next crossroads, heading back into Point of Hopes. He didn't know this part of the city as well as he knew Customs

Point, didn't dare risk the alleys for fear of being caught in a cul-de-sac. At least the whistles were receding, and he slowed his step, trying to become inconspicuous again, to blend into the thinning crowd.

In the mouth of an alley, he stopped to tie back his hair and consider his next move. Maybe the baths, he could discard his hat and coat there, acquire other in a different color—they wouldn't fit well, but that was probably to the good. And then find a street that ran parallel to Customs Road, and somehow get across Point of Hopes and Point of Knives to reach Caiazzo's house. It was just too bad this alley ended in a brick wall.

The whistles sounded again, close behind, and he broke into a trot, heading for the next intersection. Before he could reach it, a trio of pointsmen rounded the corner, truncheons drawn, and the leader pointed her at him.

"Stop right there, Eslingen."

Eslingen lifted both hands in a conciliatory gesture, and took a careful step backward. "Sorry, I think you've got the wrong man—"

They weren't buying it, and he could see why, remembered the leader from midsummer as surely as she remembered him. He turned on his heel, saw the original group coming up behind him. The wall that ended the alley was too high to climb, and there were no other outlets. His hand dropped to his knife, but he made himself let it go, lifted his hands in surrender. Surely Rathe had a plan—and if he didn't, Eslingen had a few things he could say, and prove, that would make Rathe's life just a miserable as his own.

"You'll need to come with us," the leader said. Eslingen couldn't remember her name, but he knew he'd seen her more than once during the search for the missing children.

"What's the charge?" he asked.

"Dame van Duiren claims you set on her last night," the leader answered. "It's assault for now."

Eslingen refrained from saying that if he had attacked her, she would in fact be dead. "I was nowhere near her last night," he said. "And I can prove it."

"You'll have your chance," the leader answered. Another whistle sounded behind her, and a closed carriage drew up into the street. Eslingen suppressed a sigh. He'd hoped they might walk to Point of Hopes, that there might be a chance to make a break for it, but evidently they weren't going to take any chances. One of the pointsmen held open the carriage door, and he climbed reluctantly into the scuffed interior. Another pointsman climbed in after him, followed by the leader, who stood in the door long enough to speak to the driver.

"Point of Knives, quick as you can."

"Point of Knives?" Eslingen said.

"That's where the point was called," the leader answered, and closed the door behind her. The carriage lurched into motion.

THE CELLS AT Point of Knives were surprisingly comfortable—better than Point of Hopes by a long shot, and more freshly painted than Point of Sighs. The furniture, low cot and three-legged stool, was newer, too, and Eslingen leaned back against the wall, wondering how exactly he'd managed to experience the cells in three different points stations when he'd been less than six months in the city. Nicolas Rathe, that was how, and he hoped to hell Rathe did in fact have some kind of plan. At least there was a window, set too high in the wall to reach, but it let in light and air, and the blankets looked reasonably thick. Though with any luck, he wouldn't have to spend the night.

The door at the end of the corridor opened, and he came to his feet, watching the door. Sure enough, it was Rathe who appeared, but he didn't seem to have a key in his hand, came instead to stand at the door's barred opening.

"I'm sorry about this," he said.

"I should hope so," Eslingen answered. "Haven't we played this game before?"

Rathe had the grace to look embarrassed. "It seems to happen, yes."

"It happened because you didn't tell them I was with you." Eslingen kept his voice down with an effort. He didn't really want to have this argument within the hearing of the entire station.

"There's a reason for that—"

"There'd better be a good one."

"I want to make the point on van Duiren," Rathe said.

"And nothing else matters?" Eslingen felt his voice scale up, and controlled himself sharply.

Rathe glared at him. "This is ending, right? Winter-lovers and all that? So what is there to matter?"

"Friendship? Respect? Being able to work together again?" Eslingen glared back. "Minor things like that?"

"Do you want the woman to get away with this?" Rathe demanded. "This was the best thing I could come up with at the time."

Eslingen took a breath. "Do you actually have a plan?"

"Yes." Rathe leaned against the door, grasping the bars as though he was the prisoner. "But I still need your help."

"Of course you have a plan." Eslingen turned away, shaking his head.

"I do," Rathe said.

"Well?"

"With you arrested, and me presumably cowed—because she knows damn well where we were last night—she's gotten rid of the only people who have real incentive to keep her from getting the gold," Rathe said promptly. "So we make your arrest known, and then you and I wait to see what she does. And stop her when she recovers the gold."

Eslingen stared at him. "That's your plan."

"Yeah." Rathe shrugged, one corner of his mouth turning up in a wry smile. "I didn't say it was brilliant, I said it was what I had."

There was a little silence, and then Eslingen shook his head, his mouth twitching into an answering grin. "Damn it, Nico. All right, I'm in."

"Thank you," Rathe said, and pushed himself away from the door.

"Hey, wait!" Eslingen pointed to the lock. "Aren't you going to let me out?"

"Not yet," Rathe answered. "Philip, it needs to look real. I'll bring you dinner from Amanto's."

"And a bottle of good wine," Eslingen called after him, but the pointsman was gone. Eslingen shook his head, not sure whether he wanted to laugh or curse. Only Rathe, he thought, and settled himself to wait.

RATHE PAID FOR a better dinner than he could generally afford, had it delivered to Eslingen's cell as a token of apology. He didn't quite have the courage to see how it was received, however, and concentrated instead on his own plans. Mirremay was happy enough to loan him apprentice and runners, enough to set a careful watch on van Duiren, but for the bulk of the day she stayed close to home. Her own physician came and went—looking annoyed, the runner reported—and various large young men were making their presence known at the doors, but otherwise she was staying home and resting, as one would expect after an attack.

"Which does make me wonder just a bit," Mirremay said, with a thoughtful look at Rathe. They sat in her workroom at opposite ends of the long table, a pile of slates and scraps of papers between them.

Rathe shrugged, refusing to be goaded. "Eslingen wasn't knifing Dame van Duiren last night, chief. I can attest to that."

She looked for a moment as though she was going to make an obscene quibble, then shook her head. "Be that as it may, she's not exactly doing anything actionable now. In fact—"

"I know," Rathe said. "She's doing exactly what you'd predict." He pushed himself away from the table. "But this is her best chance to get at either the gold itself, if she knows where it is, or whatever it is that tells her where Old Steen hid it."

"That's pushing it, Rathe," Mirremay said. "All the papers, hers and Caiazzo's, have been impounded by the judge."

"Not all of them," Rathe said. "Dame Lulli—she was Grandad's landlady—she had papers that belong to both of them. I sealed them in Grandad's room, and they've not been sent for. The judge said to leave them there."

"You're sure?" Mirremay asked.

Rathe nodded. "I sent a runner to double check. I've warned Dame Lulli, and she's taking herself and her people off for the night, leaving the house for us. That's where I think van Duiren's going."

"You'd better be right," Mirremay said.

"I know," Rathe said, and let himself out of the workroom. And if he did find gold or the key to it—what then? He couldn't just let Eslingen take it, though in many ways that might be the least complicated solution; he didn't really want to let Mirremay claim the reward, either, but she would be in her rights to claim a share, and Monteia wouldn't stand against her. It might be better if he didn't find anything, except that then it would be hanging over their heads, missing gold ready to cause trouble…. He shook his head. There was one more errand to run before he could release Eslingen and set his trap, and he couldn't pretend he was looking forward to it. But the tower clock was striking three, and there wouldn't be time to get to Customs Point and back before dark if he didn't hurry.

Caiazzo's house was expensively plain, the stone corner pieces brought by barge from Courtheim, the wood of the door polished *mahara* from the Silklands, the brass fittings beautifully cast and scrupulously polished. As always, Rathe felt even more disheveled than usual as he turned the bell-key, and drew himself up to his full height as a maid neat as a pin drew the door back. Caiazzo was southriver born, for all his current wealth; they were two of a kind.

"Adjunct Point Rathe, to see Master Caiazzo."

She bobbed the slightest of curtsies. "Yes, Adjunct Point, he was expecting you."

I was afraid he might be. Rathe swallowed the words as too revealing, and followed her up the broad central stair to Caiazzo's workroom.

Caiazzo's clerk hurried past them on the landing, and Rathe was unsurprised to find the merchant venturer alone in the paneled workroom. The afternoon light slanted in the long windows, warming the space and raising the smell of beeswax from the polished wood.

"So," Caiazzo said. He was standing at one end of the counter, very neat in an expensive suit of dark green wool. His hair was cropped as short as a working man's, incongruously so, but then, Rathe thought, Caiazzo was always a practical man. "I hear you've called a point on the man I sent to help you."

Words and tone were unexpectedly moderate, but Rathe still took a moment to consider his answer. "I did," he said at last.

"You can't be serious."

"I'm not," Rathe said. That earned a lifted eyebrow.

"Go on."

"You've heard this already," Rathe said.

Caizzo grinned. "In point of fact, I have, or at least some of it. But I'd like to hear your version."

"It's simple enough," Rathe said. "I want the person who killed Grandad and his son. If it's not van Duiren, though I think it is, she knows who did it. If she thinks your knife is out of the picture, she'll make her move—she has to, because she's not going to win the court case."

"No more is she," Caiazzo said. "But what makes you so sure the courts haven't already impounded whatever it is she's looking for?"

"If they had, she'd be trying to make a deal with you," Rathe said.

Caiazzo nodded slowly. "Fair enough. So what brings you to me?"

"Three things," Rathe said. "First, I wanted to tell you myself what had happened with Philip—with Eslingen."

"Which I appreciate," Caiazzo said.

"And I wanted to warn you that tonight might be a good time to stay at home, among witnesses. I'd very much prefer that your presence be accounted-for, so van Duiren can't make any wild claims."

"That's very…tactful," Caiazzo said.

Rathe shrugged. "I want a clean point, or I wouldn't bother. And I am serious. Whatever she's after, you're better off not involved, and with an alibi that even your own advocates couldn't break."

"I always take you seriously, Adjunct Point," Caiazzo said. "And I promise you, I won't be anywhere that Dame van Duiren can complain of." He paused. "So. That's two. What's your third?"

"You paid Eslingen's bond to keep his pistols here," Rathe said. "I want them. And his shot and powder."

Caiazzo's narrow eyebrows rose sharply, but he moved to the end of the table, rang a silver bell that was standing there. A few moments later, an older man appeared—the house steward, Rathe guessed. Caiazzo reached under his coat, came up with a small ring of keys.

"Go to Lietenant Eslingen's rooms, and bring back the case of pistols he keeps there."

The steward bowed stiffly and disappeared again. Caiazzo looked at Rathe.

"Is that necessary?"

"I hope not," Rathe answered. "But…."

"In that case," Caiazzo said, "I will be doubly careful to stay out of your way."

The steward returned with a polished wooden box, bound in brass and fitted with a solid lock.

"I'd open it for you," Caiazzo said, with irony, "but Eslingen has the only key."

"I'm shocked" Rathe answered, and Caiazzo lifted a hand, acknowledging the hit.

"Don't get my knife killed, Rathe. He's actually good at his job."

The steward led Rathe back to the main door—no one was going to leave him unobserved for a moment in Caiazzo's house, no matter how much their interests currently ran parallel—and he tucked the box under his arm, wondering if it was obvious to everyone that he was carrying a brace of pistols. At least Caiazzo seemed inclined to take him seriously, and that meant that he and Eslingen could concentrate on stopping van Duiren—although there was something about Caiazzo's attitude that left him worried. The man was always cocksure, but rarely this calm about something that touched his business so nearly, and he'd given up the pistols far too quickly. Was this all some plan of his? Had he already given orders for Eslingen to kill the woman if he got a chance?

Rathe shook his head. That wasn't outside of possibility, at least not where Caiazzo was concerned, but he couldn't see Eslingen going along with it. And murder was business for an outside knife anyway, with no household ties, not the public bodyguard. Still, he couldn't quite shake the feeling that he was missing something.

DINNER HAD ARRIVED with a table and chair, and an unlocked door so that Eslingen had access to the necessary without having to shout for a guard. Of course, the door at the end of the wing of cells was still locked, so it was a cheap concession, but he wasn't going to complain too loudly. At least not until Rathe was there to listen.

He cut himself another sliver of the onion tart, less because he was hungry than because he was bored, and set it down untasted as he heard the outer door open. A moment later, Rathe pushed open the cell door. Eslingen's eyes went instantly to the familiar box under his arm.

"You're expecting trouble?"

"I think we should be prepared." Rathe's tone was grim.

Eslingen lifted an eyebrow at that, but took the box, reached into his purse for the key. "Maybe you should explain what you have in mind," he said, and seated himself on the foot of the bed.

"I think she's going to break into Dame Lulli's tonight," Rathe said. "That's the place she can get at that she hasn't searched."

"Then shouldn't we be searching it first?" Eslingen asked. He opened the box, took out the pistols and the powder flask.

"We'll do that, yes," Rathe said. "Now that Mirremay's given me permission to break the seals. But I want van Duiren."

Eslingen folded the patch around the ball and rammed it home. "Just you and me?"

Rathe nodded. "Mirremay isn't that convinced I'm right. And van Durien fee'd her to look after her interests."

"That seems awfully convenient," Eslingen said. He rammed home the second ball, and checked to be sure both weapons were safely at half-cock.

"Yes, Mirremay would prefer that any awkward consequences fall on me," Rathe said. "And, no, she's not going to send us at the head of half-a-dozen strong points. Thus the pistols."

"Right," Eslingen said. "I can't say that I'm reassured."

"At least we can be sure Caiazzo won't be in the way," Rathe said, and snagged a piece of the tart.

"Oh?"

"I told him what we were doing," Rathe said, somewhat indistinctly. "And told him to stay home."

"Let's hope he does it," Eslingen said.

"If he doesn't, then any points called are his own damn fault," Rathe said.

They made their way to Dame Lulli's house as the day-sun was brushing the tops of the houses, their shadows stretching long behind them. Lulli herself was waiting at the alley door, let them in to the back garden.

97

She looked both weary and afraid, Eslingen thought, and Rathe treated her with care.

"Grandad's room is as you left it, Adjunct Point," she said, as she led them down the dark hallway. "And since you chased off the bailiffs, no one's made inquiries, bar a woman from the judge. But I've kept my man on duty day and night, and hired a second to help him."

"That's probably why you haven't had any trouble," Rathe said, with a fleeting smile.

"At what I'm paying him, I should hope so," Lulli answered. "Do you want the loan of one or both of them? You might find them useful."

"No, thanks," Rathe answered. "It's better if we keep it a points matter."

"As you please," Lulli said. She fished under her skirts, and came up with a ring of keys. "This is for all the house," she said, and began to name them, Rathe nodding attentively. Eslingen let his attention wander, surveying the parlor and the other rooms off the hall. The house was sturdily built, not the sort of place where the mere thrust of a pike could break open the shutters, and he allowed himself to relax just a little. If Rathe were right about van Duiren's plans—and that was his job, to know what people like her would do—they stood a decent chance of stopping her, particularly if they could take her by surprise.

Eslingen watched from the back door as Rathe escorted Lulli to the alley gate, and then barred the door behind him as he returned. The bar looked sturdy, and he looked at Rathe.

"I thought you wanted her to get in."

"I do." Rathe tested the bar, and nodded. "But we can't make it look too easy. A burglar's jemmy will lift that without much trouble."

"If you say so," Eslingen said, and Rathe grinned.

"It's a bit like my universal key. You have to be a bit of a specialist to want one, but—they do work."

Eslingen shook his head. "Now what?"

"First we get set up," Rathe said. "And then we take a look at Grandad's things."

Grandad's room was toward the back of the house, across from the pantry. It had probably once been a second storeroom, Eslingen guessed, but it was a convenient place to put a man who minded the door and lit the first fires in the mornings. The lock was covered with a huge blob of wax, marked with an imperfect impression of the seal on Rathe's truncheon. Rathe lit the dark lantern, though he left the shutters open, and drew his knife, holding the blade to heat in the flame.

"Another unsuspected talent," Eslingen said. He slipped his pistols out of the bag that had concealed them, and checked the priming powder.

"Don't tell me you never stole anything in all your days soldiering," Rathe said.

"We never worried about hiding our tracks," Eslingen said.

"I suppose you wouldn't, at that," Rathe said. He held the knife's blade close to his palm to test the temperature, then slid it behind the knot of wax. The hot blade slid a little way and then stuck. Rathe pulled it free, reheated it, and tried again. It took a dozen passes, heating and reheating the blade, before the wax gave way. Rathe caught it in his cupped hand and set it carefully aside. He looked into the room, checking that the shutters were still sealed, and then picked up the lantern. Eslingen followed him into the room, one pistol in his belt, the other ready in his hand.

The space was definitely a converted storeroom, still smelling faintly of candles and Silklands spice. It was comfortably furnished, a curtained bed wedged into one corner, a chest at its foot, and there was a small table and a pair of chairs against the opposite wall. Their paint was shabby, but the cushions were new, as were the bedcurtains and the neatly folded blankets. His house altar was a traveling shrine hanging above the table, the double doors folded shut. Eslingen opened them carefully, saw without surprise that small statues of Oriane and Seidos flanked an incense burner shaped like the Sea-bull. A small candelabrum stood on the table, and a lamp hung at the head of the bed: ship-shape, Eslingen thought, every inch of space put to good use, and everything tucked carefully away.

Rathe was already kneeling by the chest, universal key in hand, and a moment later lifted the heavy lid. There was a tray inside, and Rathe lifted it out, checked quickly through the clothes below it before lowering the lid gently into place.

"Nothing else in there," he said, and rose to set the tray on the table.

Eslingen set his pistol aside and lit the candles, and together they went through the miscellany that Grandad had accumulated. Most of it was unimportant—a few pieces of jewelry, an ivory statue of a Silklands dancer, one foot cracked and broken, an oiled purse that held a handful of larger coins—and Rathe shook his head.

"Nothing."

"The papers?" Eslingen pointed to a bundle tied with blue string, but Rathe was already picking at the knot.

"They look like letters," he said, and spread them on the table. "No, hang on, I've got some contracts here, old ones—and I think these are charts. Take a look."

Eslingen took the packet eagerly, unfolded the sheets in the overlapping circles of the candle's light. "Charts, yeah, but for Silklands ports. Nothing in Astreiant—nothing even in Chenedolle." He folded them back together, frowning. "Young Steen said his father didn't make maps."

"I know," Rathe said. He shook his head. "And it looks like he meant it. Nothing here that's of any use." He retied the string around the bundle. "But if Old Steen wasn't leaving something with his father, why kill the old man?"

"Because he was a witness?" Eslingen asked.

"If you wanted to avoid witnesses, all you'd have to do was wait until Old Steen left the yard," Rathe said. "That way you wouldn't have to worry about someone in the house seeing you. There has to be something here."

Unless you've gotten it all wrong, Eslingen thought, but that was something he couldn't say. Rathe frowned again, staring at the accumulation of material, then reached for the pouch of coins. He spread them out on the table, turning them each heads up, and in spite of himself Eslingen leaned closer. They were mostly larger silver coins, and mostly foreign, a pair of Chadroni demi-marks, silver staters from half the cities of the League, and Rathe picked out the gold, sliding them away from the others. It was a tidy hoard, Eslingen thought: a Silklands gold-pillar as long as a finger-joint, a notched Chadroni kingsmark, an Altheim stater that looked bright and new. Even as he frowned at the thought, Rathe reached for the stater, turning it in the light.

"This is it," he said. "Look, no customs mark."

Eslingen took it from him. Sure enough, the stamp was missing, and he cocked his head at Rathe. "All right, this may well be from Old Steen's cargo—"

"I'd lay money it is," Rathe said. "The other coins are all marked."

"But what good is one coin?" Eslingen handed it back.

"Doctrine of Resonances," Rathe said. "The part can stand for the whole, right?"

"Right." Eslingen knew he sounded doubtful.

"I've seen this before," Rathe said. "With the right spell—which I don't know, but any competent magist can deduce, it's a well-known class of spells—you can use one object of a group to lead you to all the others. This one coin will lead us to the rest."

"Then let's pack this up, and go find it." Eslingen knew before the words were out of his mouth that Rathe wouldn't buy it, but he went on anyway. "Come on, Nico, surely the most important thing is to secure this untaxed gold before some dubious magist tries to turn it into cut-rate aurichalcum."

"The most important thing is catching the person who killed Grandad and Old Steen," Rathe said. "And if that wasn't van Duiren, she knows who did."

And without the coin, no one else would be able to find the missing chest. Eslingen nodded. "All right."

They put the room to rights and blew out the candles before retreating to the hallway. Rathe busied himself reapplying the wax seal to the door—not a perfect job, Eslingen thought, but it would certainly pass in the dim light. He turned to the storeroom, pushed back the door, pleased to find the hinges well-oiled, and looked inside. There was no window, but there were counters where they could wait, and with the door half open they had a decent view of Grandad's door. Rathe came to join him, carrying the dark lantern, and Eslingen stepped back to let him in.

"What if they come in through the windows?" he asked.

Rathe shrugged. "I doubt they will—if they're going to slip a bar, might as well use the door, it's easier. But if for some reason they do, we'll hear them. Grandad's door's only held by the wax."

That made sense. "How long do you think we'll have to wait? I don't have your experience in these matters."

"Well, if it was me," Rathe said, "I'd break in between sunset and second sunrise, when everything's nice and dark."

"Soon, then," Eslingen said, and slid the lantern's shutter closed.

Rathe's voice came out of the dark. "Yeah. So be ready."

RATHE RESTED HIS hips against the counter, every shift of weight seeming thunderous in the silence. Behind him, he heard Eslingen sigh, and then the counter creaked as it took the Leaguer's weight. He slipped his hand into his pocket again, running his thumb over the rough surface. Altheim's coins were crudely made, but this one would serve its purpose, would lead anyone who knew the spell to the missing chest and its contents. Eslingen had backed off once, but they'd have the discussion again, he knew. If he gave it to Monteia, Mirremay would claim at least a half share; if he gave it to the Surintendant—well, he'd be going over Monteia's head, depriving her of the reward, and would earn an enemy where he couldn't afford one. If only there was some way to lose the damn thing.

Eslingen would never consent to that, though, and he dragged his mind back to the moment.

Van Duiren had to be coming soon, he thought. It was getting close to second sunrise, and the winter-sun still gave enough light at this time of year that surely someone would see anyone who tried to break in through a locked alley gate. Unless she wanted to wait until much later, when she could assume everyone was abed—but the winter-sun was even brighter then, and Point of Hopes patrolled here regularly. No, by all sense, she should have been here by now.

Unless he'd gotten it completely wrong. He winced at the thought, made himself go back over his reasoning. Van Duiren wanted the gold— probably to sell it to rogue magists, but that wasn't all that important. What mattered was that she could get her hands on it, and for that, she needed the key that Old Steen had left with his father. Presumably she had known about that, or she wouldn't have killed Grandad—

He swore under his breath. There was one other way that she could get her hands on Old Steen's goods, and on all of them, not just things he'd left with his father. The court had impounded them, yes, but the marriage lines were good enough to convince; if Caiazzo hadn't posted his complaint, Young Steen's case wasn't solid enough to justify keeping a man's goods from his lawful wife. And Caiazzo—he'd agreed to stay out of things just a little too easily. What were his exact words? *I won't be any- where that Dame van Duiren can complain of.* And of course she couldn't complain of his presence, if he was meeting her at her behest.

I got it wrong. I've gotten it all wrong, and Hanselin Caiazzo is going to die because of it.

He controlled his racing thoughts, reached for the lantern and snapped the shutter open.

"What?" Eslingen slid off the counter, lifting his pistol.

"If Caiazzo was going to meet someone, make a deal, a trade, where would he go?"

"What?" Eslingen said again.

"Think, damn it!" Rathe shook himself. "Philip, I got it wrong. Van Duiren's not coming here, she's going to kill Caiazzo. How else can she get control of Old Steen's goods?"

For what seemed an eternity, Eslingen stared at him, and then Rathe saw him take a deep breath. "If Caiazzo's really meeting her—I'd guess the Snake and Staves, by the Causeway. It's a neutral spot."

Rathe swore again. That was at the easternmost edge of the city, too far to walk—maybe too far even in a low-flyer. But they had to try.

He sent Eslingen ahead to find a low-flyer, stayed just long enough to lock the doors, then headed after him. At the crossroads, he looked around, hoping against hope to see a runner or a patrolling pointsman, but there was no one in sight.

"Nico!" Eslingen leaned down from the step of a low-flyer, and Rathe caught his arm, hauled himself aboard. The low-flyer jerked into motion, and Eslingen opened the trap to give directions to the driver. Rathe saw the man nod, then heard the crack of the whip as he urged his horse to greater effort.

The streets were relatively quiet in the hour or so of darkness between sunset and second sunrise, but the docks took full advantage of the extra hours of light, and as they made their way deeper into Customs Point, the low-flyer slowed to a trot and then to a walk. Rathe swore again, leaning out the door to judge their progress. Ahead, the street was filled with stevedores, carrying frames on their backs, shifting goods from a warehouse to a dray pulled by a team of four horses. Other wagons were getting through, but not quickly, and the air was full of shouted orders and the whistle of the carters' men.

"Damn it!"

"We're not far now," Eslingen said. He opened the trap, tugged at the driver's coat. "Let us down here!"

The driver pulled the low-flyer to a rattling halt, and they scrambled out, Eslingen handing up the coins for the fare.

"Which way?" Rathe asked, and the Leaguer pointed.

"That way. Where Sorrows crosses the Customs Road."

They shouldered their way past the warehouse, Rathe quickening his pace as soon as they were clear of the crowd. The streets were still active, lamps and mage-fire glowing in about half the warehouses, merchants-venturer inventorying their final cargoes, or preparing a last run before the weather broke. Rathe could smell the river, mud and tar, and guessed the tide was on the turn.

Eslingen turned south onto Sorrows Street, away from the river and into a neighborhood where the houses were further apart and backed onto marshy fields. The Snake and Staves was a larger building, three stories with a separate stable that backed onto the marsh, but the ground floor shutters were all closed, and only a few dim lights showed in the upper windows.

"Oh, Astree," Rathe breathed. "Philip—"

"It's all right," Eslingen said. "They'll be out back."

If they're here at all. Rathe swallowed the words, and followed the Leaguer across the stable court, glad to feel dirt underfoot instead of betraying pavers. The stable, too, was closed up tight, no sign of hostlers or servants stirring anywhere.

"He's here," Eslingen said, softly, as if he'd read Rathe's mind. "Caiazzo pays for his privacy."

And paid well, too, Rathe guessed. Only a sizable sum would persuade an innkeeper to close up so thoroughly at such a relatively early hour. He only hoped it wasn't going to backfire.

Eslingen caught his sleeve, and pulled him into the shadow of the inn's side wall. "There's another barn out back, on the edge of the marsh. That's where he'll be."

"Lookouts?" Rathe asked.

"There should be," Eslingen answered, "but I don't see any."

Maybe he's not here. Rathe killed that thought, and eased closer to the inn's back wall. Sure enough, there was a small barn, perched on the edge of one of the marsh channels—an excellent way for visitors to arrive unseen, or for disposing of inconvenient things, he thought. There was a bench by the closed door, but it was empty—and then his eyes focused on the bundle that lay beneath it, half in and half out of its shadow. Frowning, he reached for his glass, and in its circle, the shadow resolved itself into a body, one leg sprawling into sight. "There was one, at least," he said, and pointed.

Eslingen swore. "I don't see anyone else," he said. "We'll have to chance it."

Chance crossing open ground in the full light of the winter-sun, Rathe thought, with no way of knowing who might be watching from within. "Lovely," he said.

Eslingen drew his pistols, brought them both to full cock, the sound of the hammers loud in the still air. "Go."

Rathe took a deep breath and launched himself from the shadows. Any second, he expected a shout, or the crack of a pistol, but he fetched up against the barn's rough wall without incident. He pressed his ear against the wood, thought he could hear muffled sounds from within, but nothing clear. He edged toward the window, but it was shuttered from the inside. He waved to Eslingen, and a moment later the Leaguer had joined him.

"Is there another way in?" Rathe asked.

"Around the back," Eslingen answered. "There's a dock...."

Of course there was, and equally surely van Duiren's men would be watching it, but it was a marginally better choice than trying to get in the main door. Rathe saw the same awareness in Eslingen's eyes, and the Leaguer shrugged.

"Let's go," Rathe said.

They slipped along the side of the building, ducking under the single window. It, too, was shut fast, shuttered from within, but there was definitely a sound of voices. Rathe cocked his head, straining to hear, but could make out nothing useful. There were two speakers, a man and a woman—at least he'd guessed right, he thought, and waved Eslingen on.

The Leaguer took two steps, and stopped abruptly, the barrel of his pistol to his lips to enjoin silence. Rathe froze, and Eslingen mouthed, "Guard."

Damn it. Rathe said softly, "How many?"

Eslingen held up a single finger. He started to take a step forward, but Rathe caught his sleeve, pulling him back into the shadows. He drew his truncheon instead, and Eslingen nodded, flattening himself further against the wall to let Rathe past. Rathe peered carefully around the corner. Yes, there he was, a big man in a sailor's short coat and wide trousers, his attention on the rising winter-sun and the channels webbing the marsh. Rathe hefted his truncheon, judging the blow, and stepped out onto the dock. The wood cracked under his step, and the man started to turn, but Rathe brought his truncheon sharply across the side of his head. The man sank with a breathy moan, and Rathe caught him before he hit the ground.

"Philip!"

Eslingen slipped forward, helped drag the man into the shadows. Rathe felt for a pulse at his neck, found one, weak and thready, and pushed himself upright. The wounded would have to wait, unless.... He looked sharply at Eslingen.

"Tell me he's not one of yours."

"Never seen him before in my life," Eslingen answered promptly, and Rathe gave a sigh of relief.

"Right, then." Rathe stepped back onto the dock and eased up to the single narrow window. The shutters were closed, but not properly latched, and he could just see a sliver of the lamp-lit room, hear the rise and fall of voices. He could see Caiazzo's magist Aicelin Denizard standing to one side, her hands lifted to show them empty and unthreatening; beyond her shoulder, he saw a flicker of something dark, probably Caiazzo's coat, but the figure stepped back out of sight before he could be sure. He could just see the edge of another woman's skirt, and a man's leather-clad shoulder, and guessed that was van Duiren and at least one henchman.

"What are you, stupid?" That was Caiazzo's voice. "Do you have any idea how closely the University is tracking gold these days?"

Rathe glanced over his shoulder. "Does the door have a bar?"

Eslingen shook his head. "Lock only."

Thank Astree for small favors. Rathe turned back to the window. Van Druien had moved slightly, and now he could see that she had a double-barreled pistol in her hand.

"I'm getting the gold," she said. "You had your chance."

She lifted her hand, and Rathe swore. "Philip! The door!"

Eslingen braced himself, and gave the door two solid kicks. The lock snapped, the door flying back, and they burst together into the room. The man in leather turned, reaching for his knife, and Rathe brought him down with a single blow of the truncheon. There was a second man, he saw, and a third, both carrying swords. Eslingen fired once, brought down the most distant man before he could draw his sword, and immediately leveled the second pistol at van Duiren.

"Don't move, Dame."

She brought the pistol up anyway, almost in reflex, then swung the barrel toward Caiazzo. Eslingen pulled the trigger, but his pistol missed fire, just a puff of smoke from the lock. Eslingen reversed it instantly, and in the same moment Caiazzo moved, one hand going to his sleeve and coming out with a thin knife. He flung it expertly, and van Duiren staggered, both barrels firing wide. She fell backwards, clawing at the knife in her throat, and lay still.

"Hold it right there," Rathe said, to the third man, who dropped his sword and lifted both hands.

"I didn't want any of this, pointsman—"

"Tie him up," Rathe said, and Eslingen hastened to obey, using the man's neckcloth to secure his hands behind his back.

"Just in the nick of time," Caiazzo said, straightening his sleeves.

"Well, I, for one, am grateful," Denizard said, and there was a definite note of reproof in her voice.

"And so am I," Caiazzo said. "But they cut it a bit close."

"If you'd mentioned you had plans beside staying home—home where you'd have been safe, by the way," Rathe said, "I might have gotten here sooner."

Caiazzo waved a hand, dismissing the subject. "And all for nothing. The bastard sank his money, and there's no telling where it's gone."

"Sank it?" Rathe asked.

"There was a note in his effects," Caiazzo said.

"Which neither of you was supposed to have access to," Rathe said.

"Oh, really, Adjunct Point." Caiazzo grinned, unrepentant. "You can't expect anyone to take that seriously."

"Yes, actually, I do," Rathe said.

Caiazzo ignored him. "There was a note for his son, warning him to keep his nose out of the business because he—Old Steen—had sunk the chest in the marshes." He glanced at the broken door, the channels beyond, and shook his head. "It's lost for good, I'm afraid."

Rathe could feel the coin, a weight in his pocket, caught Eslingen giving him a wary look. He returned a stern glare, willing him to keep silent, and said, "Pity, that. But at least no one's going to stand a point tonight." He looked at Denizard. "Magist, would you rouse the house? Have them send someone to Customs Point, tell them to send as many men as they can spare."

"At once," Denizard said. She stepped over van Duiren's body, unlocked the front door, and disappeared into the dark.

"Master Caiazzo, if you'll wait here." Rathe moved toward the back door, and Caiazzo lifted his head.

"Eslingen. Go with him."

"Absolutely," Eslingen said.

Rathe walked out onto the dock, all too aware of Eslingen at his side, stopped at the end, where the water still lapped against the pilings.

"You've got the damn coin," Eslingen said. "Give it to him."

"I can't." Rathe shoved his hands into his pockets, feeling the metal rough under his fingers. "Philip, you know I can't."

"He's going to use it to fund his caravans," Eslingen said. "You know that."

"Yes, probably, though there's nothing to stop him selling it to the magists—" Rathe stopped, silence by Eslingen's lifted eyebrow. "All right, yes, he'll fund his caravans. It's still illegal."

"So are you going to give it to Mirremay?" Eslingen demanded. "That would be utterly and entirely legal, and she'd use the reward to make her little fiefdom even stronger. But that would be according to the law."

"It would be," Rathe said. The gold was lost, sunk in the marsh where it was unlikely anyone would find it except by happenstance. He could afford to lose the key as well. He turned the coin over again, slipped it from his pocket. It glinted dully in the winter-sun's light, a disk no wider than the joint of his thumb. He squinted into the dark, seeing the pale glimmer of light on the water of the channels. "It would still be wrong."

He flung the coin out into the night, as far and as hard as he could throw it, saw it catch the light once, and then heard the splash as it landed somewhere in the brackish water.

"No," he said, "I'm not giving it to anybody. Let the whole damn thing stay there and rot for all I care. At least it'll do no harm."

"If Caiazzo finds out—or Mirremay—" Eslingen shook his head.

"Or Monteia, or the Surintendant," Rathe said. "Or Vair. Are you going to tell them?"

Eslingen shook his head again. "Not me. But you're a dangerous man to know, Adjunct Point."

Rathe turned back toward the barn, and Eslingen fell into step at his side. "You could stop knowing me."

"That was the agreement." Eslingen stopped abruptly, and Rathe turned back, frowning.

"What?"

"I don't particularly want to," Eslingen said.

Rathe sighed. "No more do I. It's not practical, Philip."

"We'll think of something," Eslingen said. It was more optimism than Rathe thought was warranted, but it warmed him nonetheless.

Chapter Seven
EPILOGUE

THE SURINTENDANT OF Points was not entirely displeased. Rathe clasped his hands more tightly behind his back and tried to pretend that he didn't still smell of sweat from a long hunt through the 'Serry, chasing a too-brazen pickpocket. They'd caught the girl—one of Estel Quentier's apprentices, and she'd be bailed out by now, back home with her teachers—but the summons from City Point had arrived before he'd had time to visit the baths, or even fetch a clean shirt. And the wording had made it clear that the Surintendant expected his immediate attendance.

"Dame van Duiren's surviving man confessed that his comrade had shot Old Steen when he wouldn't say what he'd done with the gold," Rathe said, "and then Grandad set on them. The other man killed Grandad, but by then they'd lost Old Steen, and the house was stirring. I think that's the last of it, sir."

"Caillavet Vair reports that she found your questions interesting, but she's disappointed in the lack of follow up." Rainart Fourie looked at the neat stack of paper on his desk. "And Head Point Mirremay has filed a formal complaint of interference in a matter that properly belonged to Point of Knives."

"I sent Maseigne everything I'd found that pointed to the University," Rathe said. "It wasn't much, but she got all I had."

"Descriptions of two magists—no, one magist and someone who might have been a member of the University—who visited Dame van Duiren," Fourie said. "Sketchy descriptions, at that."

"It was all I had," Rathe said again.

Fourie nodded. "As for Mirremay—well, I can't agree with the complaint, and I will not uphold it. However…." He looked at his papers again. "I believe it would be wise to reassign you, Rathe."

He lifted one of the sheets, and handed it across. Rathe took it warily, frowning as he read the clerk's neat hand. "Point of Dreams?"

"Senior Adjunct Point at Point of Dreams." Fourie gave a thin smile. "Trijn's been complaining that we don't give her the best people. I hope this will silence her."

Dreams took precedence over Hopes: it was a promotion, and wrapped in a compliment. Rathe shook himself, unable quite to believe what he was hearing. The silence stretched for a long moment before he found words. "Thank you, Surintendant."

Fourie waved a hand. "Go. And stay out of Point of Knives."

"Yes, Surintendant," Rathe said, and hastily effaced himself.

It still hadn't sunk in by the time he'd crossed the Hopes-Point Bridge. Senior Adjunct at a higher station—no, he hadn't expected anything like that, had thought he'd be lucky to get away with a scolding, and possibly a token fine for poaching on Mirremay's turf. Senior Adjunct at Dreams….

"Nico!"

Rathe started, looked sideways to see Eslingen beckoning from the doorway of a lace-maker's shop. "Philip?"

"Inside," Eslingen said, and Rathe followed him into the sweet-smelling shadows. "I've had a clever idea."

"Oh?" Rathe knew he sounded wary, and Eslingen grinned.

"Do you like theater, Adjunct Point?"

In spite of himself, Rathe laughed. "I'd better. I've just been reassigned to Point of Dreams."

"All the better," Eslingen said.

"Oh?" Rathe said again.

"Theaters are—mostly—in Point of Dreams," Eslingen said, sounding faintly smug. "So that will be convenient. And theaters, I've discovered, have private boxes that can be rented for a quite affordable fee. Sometimes including supper."

"Philip, you're mad."

"I have a box," Eslingen said. "For tonight's play at the Galenon. Would you care to join me?"

"So you've forgiven me for losing the key?" Rathe asked.

"I never blamed you," Eslingen answered. "Caiazzo's still not very happy about the whole situation—thus the private box."

"What's the play?" Rathe asked.

"Does it matter?"

Rathe laughed. Eslingen held out one of the slips of wood that served as the marker, and Rathe accepted it. "Now who's dangerous to know?"

Eslingen swept him a bow. "I do my level best. Until tonight, Adjunct Point."

"Until tonight," Rathe answered. The promotion would be worth it after all.

Acknowledgments

Thanks to the usual suspects: Jo Graham, Amy Griswold, Don Sakers, Thomas Atkison, Carl Cipra, the First Readers on LJ, Alex Jeffers for the design, and Ben Baldwin for the cover.

MELISSA SCOTT is from Little Rock, Arkansas, and studied history at Harvard College and Brandeis University, where she earned her PhD in the Comparative History program with a dissertation titled "Victory of the Ancients: Tactics, Technology, and the Use of Classical Precedent." She is the author of more than twenty science fiction and fantasy novels, most with queer themes and characters, and has won Lambda Literary Awards for *Trouble and Her Friends*, *Shadow Man*, and *Point of Dreams*, the last written with her late partner, Lisa A. Barnett. She has also won a Spectrum Award for *Shadow Man* and again in 2010 for the short story "The Rocky Side of the Sky" (*Periphery*, Lethe Press) as well as the John W. Campbell Award for Best New Writer. She can be found on LiveJournal at mescott.livejournal.com.